The Watch on the Fencepost

The Watch on the Fencepost

Kay DiBianca

CrossLink Publishing

CrossLink Publishing
13395 Voyager Pkwy, Ste 130
Colorado Springs, CO 80921
www.crosslinkpublishing.com

Ordering Information:
Quantity sales. Special discounts are available on quantity purchases by corporations, associations, and others. For details, contact the "Special Sales Department" at the address above.

The Watch on the Fencepost/DiBianca —1st ed.

ISBN 978-1-63357-154-9

Library of Congress Control Number: 2018951011

First edition: 10 9 8 7 6 5 4 3 2 1

This is a work of fiction. Names, characters, businesses, places, events, locales, and incidents are either the products of the author's imagination or used in a fictitious manner. Any resemblance to actual persons, living or dead, or actual events is purely coincidental.

In recognition of God's greatest gifts to me:

My husband, Frank

Our son, Arthur

My parents, Arthur and Virginia Carpenter

I dedicate this novel to them and to Him.

"The most beautiful experience we can have is the mysterious. It is the fundamental emotion that stands at the cradle of true art and true science."

—Albert Einstein, "The World as I See It"

Contents

Acknowledgments...1

Prologue..3

Chapter 1 5

Chapter 2...9

Chapter 3...13

Chapter 4...15

Chapter 5...19

Chapter 6...23

Chapter 7...27

Chapter 8...31

Chapter 9...35

Chapter 10...39

Chapter 11...43

Chapter 12...47

Chapter 13...53

Chapter 14...57

Chapter 15...59

Chapter 16 63

Chapter 17 67

Chapter 18 69

Chapter 19 73

Chapter 20 77

Chapter 21 83

Chapter 22 85

Chapter 23 87

Chapter 24 91

Chapter 25 93

Chapter 26 99

Chapter 27 103

Chapter 28 107

Chapter 29 111

Chapter 30 115

Chapter 31 121

Chapter 32 125

Chapter 33 127

Chapter 34 131

Chapter 35 135

Chapter 36 139

Chapter 37 143

Chapter 38 149

Chapter 39 155

Chapter 40 161

Chapter 41 167

Chapter 42 171

Chapter 43 173

Chapter 44 177

Chapter 45 181

Chapter 46 185

Chapter 47 189

Chapter 48 191

Chapter 49 195

Chapter 50 197

Chapter 51 203

Chapter 52 207

Chapter 53 211

Chapter 54 215

Chapter 55 217

Chapter 56 221

Chapter 57 223

Chapter 58 225

Chapter 59 229

Chapter 60 233

Chapter 61 239

Chapter 62 241

Chapter 63 245

Chapter 64 247

Chapter 65 251

ABOUT THE AUTHOR 255

Acknowledgments

I am deeply grateful for the guidance, counsel, love, and support of so many people who helped bring this book to publication:

Good friends and family who took the time to read and give feedback on all or part of various drafts: Arthur DiBianca, Glenda Higgins, Jan Keyes, Angela Mutzi, Maida Smith, and Claudio and Maria Tombazzi.

Friends and acquaintances who provided their expertise on various aspects of the novel: Dale Foster, Rabbi Mordechai Harris, Dr. Allen Raich, and Dave Tucker.

Numerous editors, agents, and publishers who offered advice and assistance along the way: especially Jennifer Pooley, who edited the first version of the book; Rachel Hills who provided an outstanding plot review; and my editor and mentor, Kathy Ide, who edited the last several versions of the book and continues to guide me in the publication phase.

And so many others who offered encouragement and prayer as I walked through this journey.

Finally, my wonderful husband, Frank, who read every manuscript version cover-to-cover and found a way to balance "This is great writing . . ." with "However . . ." in a way that simultaneously encouraged and instructed me. Thank you, Frank!

"The LORD is my strength and my shield; in Him my heart trusts, and I am helped; my heart exults, and with my song I give thanks to Him." -- Psalm 28:7

Prologue

It was almost graceful, the way it dropped over the side of the mountain and glided down toward the valley below. To an outside observer, it would have seemed to fall effortlessly on a carpet of air, like a bride's veil carried away on a gentle summer breeze.

Down and down it continued, buoyed by the cool night air, a silent conveyance seeking its destination below. No sound disturbed its swift descent until it struck an outcropping on the side of the mountain and exploded in a huge fireball.

The sound of the blast could be heard ten miles away, and the impact was so severe that parts of the car flew off in all directions. By the time the emergency crew maneuvered its way through the barren desert valley without the benefit of roads, the fire that had emboldened the night sky was just a smoldering mass of aluminum and steel, hardly recognizable as an automobile at all. This would not be a rescue operation.

"Must have been a full tank of gas, the way that thing exploded," said Arnold Brewster, the crew chief, as he peered into what was left of the cab of the car. "Looks like a couple of bodies in there."

The rest of the eight-person crew gathered around the burned-out hulk.

"Lord knows, nobody will be able to identify them."

One team member kicked at the dust. "Why don't they put a guardrail along every foot of that mountain road, Arnie? These crazy tourists don't know how to drive up here."

"There are guardrails on all the curves. This guy must have driven right off the side of the straightaway."

Brewster ordered the emergency team to spread out over the area and recover anything that might be of use. "Take plenty of pictures. We want to know where every piece of this thing ended up."

The state patrol had blocked off the mountain road above them. An officer radioed down, "Hey, Arnie. There's no clue up here as to why that car went off the road. There aren't any skid marks. Looks like it just rolled off the side of the mountain."

Brewster shrugged. "Yeah. We've seen it before. The driver probably fell asleep at the wheel. Or maybe he was drunk and passed out after losing a ton of money at the poker tables. Whatever. Thanks for your help, guys. We'll take care of things down here."

Ten minutes later and two hundred yards away, a young EMT shouted as she scrounged through a scorched crater. "Hey, Arnie. I found the back bumper." The others gathered around her. "The license plate is still attached. It's half burned up, but it's readable. Maybe we can ID these folks through the car information."

Arnie gave a crisp nod and addressed the crew. "Okay. Continue looking and see if you can find anything that might be useful." He sighed and murmured under his breath, "Not that it'll help the next of kin. They're gonna have a real hard time dealing with this."

CHAPTER 1

Monday

"C'mon Barkley. Keep up. We're training for a marathon, not a stroll in the garden." Halfway through her five-mile run at Campbell Park, Kathryn Lee Frasier glanced back at her little sable-colored border collie who had stopped to investigate a twig by the side of the trail. Hearing her call, Barkley bounded back to his owner's side, gleefully yipping in the late afternoon chill.

Winter had been slow to loosen its grip on the western foothills of the Rockies this year, and Kate could taste the arctic-forged air as it drove deep into her lungs. Her breath puffed out frosty little clouds each time she exhaled, keeping time with her strides. "Let's pick up the pace," she said as she dodged a patch of snow.

Campbell Park, or "Runners' Heaven" as the locals called it, was like an old friend to Kate. She had trained on its trails when she ran cross-country in high school, and she knew every rise and fall, every switchback, and every level path in the place. But for the past month, this park had taken on new meaning.

"Let's go, Barkley. Up the hill." She tucked a strand of dark hair back under her fleece headband, and the two galloped together past the three-mile marker and up a slight incline to the highest point in the park, where the trail overlooked the town of Bellevue.

Bellevue was one of those adolescent towns that had sprouted out of the hip of a larger, more mature city to its east. Spurred on by some kind of urban hormones, it continued to develop enthusiastically without the burdens of old infrastructure, old industries, or old ideas. But, like most teenagers, it probably thought a little more of itself than it should have and gave less attention to the wisdom of its elders than it could have.

As a matter of fact, if an airplane flew over the town and dropped one hundred leaflets out, half of them would land in the yards of large homes with a swimming pool or a children's cedar activity center in the backyard and a BMW in the driveway. But most of the remaining half would land on smaller properties owned by the "old-timers," those folks who made their livings in Bellevue when it was just a country village and who now provided many of the support services for their new neighbors.

As they passed the four-mile marker, Kate began to pay a price for setting a strong pace early. "Almost there, Barkley," she said. Then to herself: *Never give up.*

Never give up. Her mantra for the past month since Reverend Whitefield suggested the marathon. The Whitefields had always been her spiritual guides. Now they were shepherding her through the darkness.

"Mourning for your parents is very important, Kathryn, but you can't let it take over your life," the reverend had said. "It's been three months since the accident, and this would be an appropriate time for you to find something to focus your attention on as you continue to deal with the sorrow. You're a runner. Have you ever considered training for a marathon?"

"No. I've never had the time or the courage to take on a full marathon."

But the good reverend and his wife knew her too well. She could never refuse a challenge.

"It won't be easy," Jan Whitefield had said. "I've run several marathons myself, and I can tell you that the training will test your mental and physical capabilities to the limit."

It would be demanding, but that's what she wanted. Something physical. And hard. Her manager at Vectra Software Corporation had given her a long-term leave of absence. So why not?

And so she ran. And as the miles built up, the sorrow began to fade. And her old sense of well-being was rekindled.

Kate and Barkley turned into the wind as they rounded the last bend in their route. The raw air slapped her in the face and made her eyes leak tears. Her body demanded that she slow down, but she pushed back against the desire to relieve the pain in her legs and concentrated on the soft *thump, thump* of her Sauconys on the paved path.

With a quarter mile to go, her thighs were on fire and her breaths had become short, savage gasps. She clenched her fists for the final sprint. "Race you to the finish, Barkley," she wheezed out as she drove to the end.

Finally, it was over, and they were back at the beginning of the trail, next to a park bench. Lungs burning, she bent over, hands on her knees, to catch her breath. With her chest still heaving from the effort, she leaned down and ruffled Barkley's pert little ears. "We made it. Good boy."

As the sun sank into the hills, a park ranger rode by on a bicycle. "We're closing in a few minutes—time to wrap it up," he said as he headed down the trail to find other stragglers.

She waved to him. "No problem. I just have to stretch out." Kate put her hands on the park bench and extended each leg alternately behind her until the muscles slowly relaxed their tension.

When she stood upright and pulled a deep breath of cold air into her lungs, something caught her eye. Behind the park bench, on top of an old fencepost, a tiny gold object glittered with light from the setting sun. A watch on the fencepost.

CHAPTER 2

P hil Warren laid the monthly reports aside and checked his watch. *Five-thirty. Just about time for Ben's daily debrief.*

"Evenin', sport." Ben Mullins strolled into Phil's office, put his coffee cup on the desk, and settled into a chair opposite his boss.

"Good evening, Ben." Phil took a sip from his water bottle and scrutinized the face of his good friend, wondering what today's topic would be. For the past ten years, the two men had met regularly after a hard day's work to unwind and discuss everything from the state of the business to the latest football scores.

"So, what's happening?" Phil asked.

Ben ran a hand through his dark, buzz-cut hair. He looked older than his thirty-eight years. And yet, despite his deeply lined and weathered face, he had an intelligent air about him, which he tried to hide behind a folksy, approachable facade. Few people would have guessed that he held a master's degree in mechanical engineering from Purdue University or that he was extremely well read, especially in nineteenth-century English literature. Trim and athletic, he was the one employee who was allowed to interact with the boss on an even playing field.

"Not much to report." Ben leaned back in his chair with his legs stretched out in front of him, his cowboy boots crossed at the ankles. "Mrs. Widner brought her Cadillac in again today for an oil change. I keep tellin' her she doesn't need to change the oil every month, but she keeps bringing it back in. She says she wants her car to be as clean on the inside as it is on the outside." Ben grimaced. "Now why do you suppose a smart woman like Mrs. Widner would say something as silly as that?"

"No idea."

"Well, I have a theory." Ben almost always had a theory. "See, she and her husband are new in town. I hear he travels a lot, and their kids are all grown up and living in other parts of the country. I've told her we can have someone drive her home, but she always chooses to sit in the waiting room and talk to the other customers. I think she's lonely." He shook his head. "Awful expensive way to make new friends."

And an awful long dissertation on Mrs. Widner and her Cadillac, Phil thought. *I wonder what's really on his mind.*

There was a protracted silence as Ben brushed at a piece of lint on his blue jeans; then he picked up a car magazine and flipped through the pages. Clearly, he was waiting to be asked.

Okay, I'll bite. "Anything else you want to talk about?"

Ben dropped the magazine back on the table next to his chair and showed that little lopsided smile of his that meant he was getting to the crux of the matter. "Oh, nothin' much. But I was just checkin' the schedule for the rest of the week, and I noticed Kathryn Frasier is bringing her car in on Thursday for some maintenance work."

Ah, so that's it. "So?"

"Yep. Ten o'clock Thursday morning. Knowin' her, she'll be right on time too. Did you ever notice how nicely organized and punctual she is?"

"No, I never noticed that." Phil watched the lines around Ben's blue eyes deepen as his grin widened.

"Well, I just want to be sure you're aware of what's goin' on around here. Maybe you could spiff up a little bit before she comes. You know, try to make a good impression. After all, she's the only female who comes in this place who doesn't throw herself at you."

Phil leaned back in his chair and put his hands behind his head. "Thanks for the advice, pal. Coming from the oldest bachelor in Bellevue, I'll take it for what it's worth. In the meantime, maybe you should spend a little less time worrying about my personal life and a little more time thinking about how we can boost our throughput."

Ben retrieved his cup from Phil's desk. "I'd say both things need some improvement," he chuckled, then took a last swallow of coffee and tossed the paper cup into the wastebasket. "Speaking of improvement, have you ever read anything by Jane Austen?"

"No. I'm more of a Jack London kind of guy."

"It's educational to read a book written by a woman. Did you know that women think differently than men?"

"Yeah. Everybody knows that." *I wonder where this is going.*

"Well, it's real interestin' to get inside the head of a woman. Austen makes a good case about how men and women don't communicate effectively with each other. You could learn something from her. Try reading *Pride and Prejudice.* Might just give you a little useful insight."

Phil went back to analyzing his paperwork.

"See, Mr. Darcy and Elizabeth Bennett got off to a real bad start, and they spent so much time making assumptions about each other, they almost missed the most important thing of all."

Phil looked up. "And what's the most important thing of all?"

"Read the book and you'll find out." Self-satisfaction etched itself into the lines on Ben's face.

Phil responded, "Hmph."

Ben stood and stretched. "Well, I guess I'll head on out. You coming to the gym tonight? Bet I can still whip your rear end at racquetball."

"Yeah, I'll be there. You better go start warming up right now, old man, so you can get that decrepit body of yours in shape for a game."

Ben exited the office, whistling.

Should I tell him? thought Phil. *No. Not yet.*

CHAPTER 3

Kate reached over the park bench and gently lifted the watch from the fencepost. The dainty timepiece had several tiny diamonds speckled around its rectangular face. The thin, flexible band had a small chain to protect it from accidentally unlatching and falling off. Somebody must have deliberately removed it and put it on the fencepost.

Kate glanced around. Surely the owner must be close by. But there was no one in sight, and hers was the only car in the parking area next to the trail. This near closing time, especially late on a winter day, the park was virtually deserted.

"Look at this, Barkley. I'm holding time in my hands." *What was it Professor Adkins used to say?* "With time all things are revealed." She held the watch up at eye level to get a closer look in the fading light. "So, little watch, what story do you have to tell?"

All the watch said was the time: three o'clock. Kate compared it with her wrist-mounted GPS, which read five-thirty. *An expensive watch that doesn't even keep correct time.*

She turned the watch over and found an inscription on the back: "To Cece - 1998." *My goodness. That was twelve years ago. This Cece should take better care of her things.*

Barkley woofed, reminding her it was time to go. After looking around once more and finding no one in sight, she drove to the visitor's center. She parked her car and glanced at the watch again. It still read three o'clock. *Battery must be dead, but that's no reason to take a watch off and leave it in the park.*

As she got out of her car, the frigid air chilled the sweat on the back of her neck, and she realized how cold she was. She grabbed a heavy jacket from the back seat. "Stay, Barkley. I'll be right back."

She walked into the center and up to the information desk. "Do you have a lost and found department?" she asked the middle-aged lady who was sitting there.

"Yes, we do," said the woman. "People are leaving things in the park all the time. We have jackets, gloves, hats. Last week someone even came across a wedding ring lying on the ground in the parking lot!"

Kate held up the watch. "I just found this on a fencepost over by the Sunset Trail."

The lady took the watch and checked it out. "What a lovely watch. And it looks expensive. I'll put it in the safe. If the owner comes in to reclaim it, she'll have to describe it before we'll hand it over. I see there's an inscription on the back. She'll have to identify that too." She took out a small plastic bag and dropped the watch in it. "Thank you for bringing it in. I'm sure the owner will be very happy to get it back."

As Kate drove home, the thought of the little timepiece tickled her imagination. Why would someone take off an expensive watch and reach over the bench to put it on top of an old fencepost? Even a tall person would have a hard time reaching the post from there.

A puzzle, she thought.

When she was a child, her father often gave her little problem-solving challenges, saying, "Puzzles are our friends. Solve a puzzle and you're one step closer to ultimate truth. Solve a puzzle and you're one step closer to God."

She smiled broadly, the first time she'd felt this sense of curiosity in months. "Well, Barkley, I doubt I'll solve this puzzle." *But, on the other hand . . .*

CHAPTER 4

It's way too quiet in here.

Mike Strickland walked into campaign headquarters and looked around at the dozen or so workers in the outer office. *This place should be buzzing with activity, but these people look about as dull as dishwater.*

His candidate, US Representative Robert Hodges, had announced months ago that he would run for governor, and the organization was now in place, but where was the enthusiasm? *Can we make this happen?*

Mike spoke what he hoped were inspiring words to a few of the workers on his way to the office where the meeting was scheduled.

"Afternoon, folks," he said as he took his seat on one side of the small conference table. The other two members of the senior staff were already there, settled in their places.

Elizabeth Howley sat opposite him. *The Dragon Lady.* Of the three members of the senior staff, she was the oldest and most experienced. And ruthless. But Hodges relied on her unconditionally. Rumor had it she'd already picked out her office in the governor's mansion and hired a decorator to design the furnishings.

Liz looked up from her laptop and smoothed her hair back with a perfectly manicured hand. "Hello, Mike. How's the fundraising coming along?"

"Good. We got a few pledges today."

The campaign manager sat next to Elizabeth. If Liz Howley was intense and dominant, Jeremy Dodd was downright crafty. Mike had argued against hiring him since he had never run a campaign before, but Hodges had overruled him. It wasn't just the experience thing that bothered Mike. Jeremy didn't seem to have any commitment to the issues. A successful campaign would be a major stepping stone for him, and he would bend his values in any direction as long as it gave him the win. *A chameleon with a bad haircut.*

Jeremy looked up under heavy black eyebrows and acknowledged Mike's presence with a nod. Then he continued scribbling notes on the papers in front of him.

Mike got up to get a bottle of water from the small refrigerator at the end of the room and returned to his seat. "Where's Bob?" he asked.

"He stepped out to take a phone call. He should be back in a minute," Liz responded and went back to tapping on her laptop.

Representative Hodges strode energetically into the room. "Mike, I'm glad you're here in time for our meeting." The two men shook hands, and Hodges took his place at the head of the table. "Guys, I just talked to former governor Sparks, and I'm happy to tell you he's going to endorse me at the rally in Bellevue on Saturday."

After a round of congratulations, Hodges rubbed his hands briskly together. "Okay, let's get down to business. Jeremy, how's the campaign going?"

"We're making progress," Jeremy said.

That's about the best face you can put on it, Mike thought.

Jeremy walked around the table and laid a spreadsheet in front of his candidate. "Look," he said, pointing to a column of numbers. "You're still a few points down in the polls . . ."

A few? Since when is ten points a few?

". . . and Steve the Gray Man is running all around the state claiming he has this election in the bag." *Steve the Gray Man* was the epithet Jeremy liked to saddle on Hodges's opponent, Steve Grayson.

Hodges put on his reading glasses and studied the polling data Jeremy had handed him. "Somebody should tell Grayson you're supposed to boast about your success when you're taking your armor off, not when you're putting it on," he muttered.

Mike nodded. "Amen to that."

Hodges took off his reading glasses and let them hang on a cord around his neck. "I know we started this campaign at a disadvantage, but I'm confident we can overtake Grayson on the issues. What I'm worried about is his tendency to play dirty. He beat Lamar Meredith for that state senate seat by digging up some insignificant tax problem Lamar had years ago. Grayson made an issue out of it and made it stick. We have to watch him. Mike, what do you think?"

Mike crossed one ankle over the other knee. In the five years he'd been chief of staff, he had learned that Robert Hodges wasn't looking for good news. He wanted to identify potential problem areas in the campaign, weaknesses that could be exploited by the competition. "The polls haven't shifted much since you announced your candidacy, and potential donors are waiting to see if your message is going to resonate with the voters before they commit." He looked pointedly at Jeremy. "We need to find some way to kick-start this campaign."

"Liz?" Hodges turned to his personal assistant.

Liz pursed her lips together. "Every campaign is different, and this one looks like it's going to be a real fight. We can't afford even a small setback. If we hear of any story that might surface to hurt us, we need to slap it down hard." She slammed the table top with the palm of her hand so ferociously that Jeremy's pen fell on the floor.

Note to self: don't ever cross that woman.

Hodges rested his elbows on the table. "I believe Bellevue is the key to this campaign. It's a natural constituency for me. If we build a strong base of support there, we can spread our success to the rest of the state. Let's focus our energy on the good folks in Bellevue, but we still need to keep an eye on Grayson. Liz, I'll depend on you to stay in touch with your contacts in Grayson's campaign so we don't get blindsided by anything."

"Will do."

Hodges pulled a copy of the weekly schedule out of his pocket and examined it. "The rally in Bellevue on Saturday is the cornerstone going forward. Jeremy, make sure the TV stations know about the Sparks endorsement. And see if you can get them to lead their nightly news with a story about the rally."

Jeremy picked his pen up off the floor and made a note. "I'll get right on it."

Mike checked the calendar on his phone. "We'll be in Bellevue on Thursday to meet with some of the business folks. Maybe we should drop by campaign headquarters and gin up the staff and volunteers. Get them into high gear for Saturday's rally."

"Good idea. Jeremy, get the word out to the folks in Bellevue that I'll stop by for a couple of hours on Thursday. Bellevue is a 'must have' for us, and the rally is the key."

The rally is the key, all right. If we can't create some excitement soon, we'll all be looking for new jobs.

CHAPTER 5

*W*hy would someone leave an expensive watch on a fencepost?

Kate sat on the tan leather couch in her living room with her laptop on her knees. She typed the Computerworld URL into the browser, but before the homepage appeared, she put her computer aside.

Why was the watch not keeping time? And there was something about it—something familiar. Kate had impressive powers of recall; "the steel trap" her parents had labeled it. She could remember names, faces, facts—just about anything she had come in contact with. Sometimes she had the sense of having seen something before but couldn't remember the context.

She walked over to her studio piano, sat on the bench, and began playing scales. The regular movement of her fingers up and down the keyboard and the steady, systematic change in tones helped her think. Her body swayed back and forth. She fingered several chords. Harmony, she thought. *All the pieces have to fit together.* But it wasn't working.

She stopped playing and turned around on the piano bench. "Think," she said quietly. Barkley raised his head and peered at her for a moment, then lowered it back down onto his paws.

Her father had taught her that trying to solve a troublesome problem can sometimes cause the mind to put up roadblocks. He'd always advised her to temporarily put it aside, clear her head, and relax. She went to the kitchen and got a doggie treat for the grateful Barkley. Then she made herself a cup of tea and spent several minutes stretching sore muscles.

With Barkley tapping along on the hardwood floor behind her, she paced slowly beside the bookshelves behind the couch, letting her fingertips brush along the books as she passed. She stopped in front of a set of favorite volumes she'd saved from her childhood. Nancy Drew and the Hardy Boys occupied several shelves.

She pulled out a little paperback that was well-worn by a small child's enthusiastic hands. She smiled as she flipped through the pages and put the tiny volume back in its place. *What would Big Max, the World's Greatest Detective, do?*

At the other end of the bookshelves, she scanned framed photos of her with her parents at various stages in her life. The shelf above the pictures held a row of photo albums. One sat apart from the rest. It had once been white, but the years had dulled it to a faint yellow. It held pictures of her mother's growing-up years.

Kate took the album to the couch, set her teacup on the coffee table, and opened it to the first photo of her mother as a small child—a blonde, curly-haired tyke. Successive pages showed Leah Dawson growing more beautiful with each picture and each year. The last page had Leah as a teenager standing with four friends, all wearing suits, hats, and gloves. Leah stood in the middle of the group, holding a round silver platter with both hands and smiling broadly at the camera.

Peeking out from beneath the sleeve of her mother's white suit was a watch. *Is it possible?* Kate squinted as she tried to focus, but the picture was so small she couldn't make out the details of the tiny watch.

She took the album into the kitchen and got a magnifying glass from one of the drawers. As she slowly moved the lens closer to focus in on the timepiece, her breath caught in her throat. It had a rectangular face with tiny diamonds and a thin band. Exactly like the watch she had found on the fencepost.

But how could it be? I never saw mother wear that watch. If it really was hers, it must have been lost or given away long ago.

But as she stared at the old black-and-white photo, Kate was certain the broken watch with an inscription to "Cece" was identical to the one in this picture.

If this were a Nancy Drew mystery, the story would have someone leaving the watch on the fencepost for her to find. And it would have been set to three o'clock for some purpose. But who would do that? And why?

"A mystery," Kate said out loud, and she felt her spine tingle with a mixture of excitement, curiosity, and fear. "What would Dad say about this, Barkley?" The little dog woofed in response. She could almost hear her father's voice, "We live in a rational world, Kathryn. When things don't seem to make sense, start with what you know and put the pieces of the puzzle together until you see the whole picture."

She grabbed her phone and checked her calendar for the next day. Mr. Kaplan had asked her to meet some people Tuesday evening for dinner, but the rest of the day was free. "Okay, Barkley. Let's see what happens if we return to the park and that fencepost at three o'clock tomorrow afternoon."

CHAPTER 6

Tuesday

I hope I didn't screw anything up.

Tommy Abrahams paused outside of Gavin's closed office door, wondering why his CEO had summoned him for a meeting. He tucked his rumpled shirt into his pants and wiped the sweat off his forehead.

Gavin's voice had sounded stern when he called to ask Tommy to drop by his office around two o'clock. But Gavin's voice always sounded stern to Tommy, who was more at home among the computers he maintained than with the people he worked for. Machines made more sense. They did what you told them to do. And if there was a problem, there was always a root cause that could be identified. Machines were easy to work with. People, not so much.

Tommy took a deep breath and gently knocked on his boss's door.

"Come in." Gavin Connelly looked up from behind the large desk at the far end of the room. "Have a seat, Tommy. I just need to finish one email, and I'll be right with you."

If an office could talk, this one's conversation would be calm, precise, and grammatically correct. It was a large room featuring modern, upscale furniture: a Plexiglass-topped executive desk at one end and a matching credenza at the other. A couch and several chairs were arranged in the middle of the room. Framed copies of patents awarded to the company's employees lined the walls next to black composite bookshelves.

The blinds were closed behind Gavin's desk, but the bright overhead LED lights cast shadows that magnified the unemotional simplicity of the black, white, and gray furniture. The room had all the appearances of power and progress, and it made Tommy feel awkward. Even his accomplishment of earning a degree in computer science with honors didn't offer a sense of assurance in this rarified atmosphere of corporate super tech.

Tommy walked past the couch and eased his bulk down into one of the straight chairs in front of Gavin's desk. While Gavin typed, Tommy slumped in his chair and tried to focus on his dad's views about how to succeed in business.

His father was a salty veteran of the navy and had lectured him on the necessity of following orders when he had first accepted this job. "Don't forget," he had said, "the boss is just like a ship's captain. You do what he says and he'll take care of you. Play by his rules. Follow his orders. To the letter!" And since Gavin Connelly was a rules-and-regulations kind of boss, Tommy carried the weight of his father's warning like an anchor.

Gavin was slim and serious, with thinning dark hair over a pale complexion. He was not a man given to standing around the water cooler, even if there had been one, and schmoozing with the employees. He radiated a kind of self-assured authority that made Tommy wonder if he ever perspired.

But Tommy admired Gavin. Envied him. He had the kind of life any engineer-type would covet. His father had founded the company and set Gavin up as CEO a couple of years ago. It was a plum job. After all, how much oversight did it take to run a company that consisted of a bunch of self-starting engineers whose jobs were to invent and patent new products that they would receive part of the profits from?

"Thanks for waiting. These emails are taking over my life." Gavin glanced up from his work and gave a little nod. "So, Tommy, how's everything going?"

Tommy flinched. *I wonder what this is all about.* "Fine. No problems."

"That's good to hear. I just wanted to follow up on that issue we had with our email server. I think you said we lost a year's worth of backups. Were you able to recover them?"

Oh, so that's it. He still blames me for the email server crash. He brings it up every time we talk even though it happened months ago. "No. It was a really strange thing. Like I told you before, I got paged from the system that the server had gone down. It happens occasionally, but when I rebooted, it looks like a whole section of emails just vanished. Close to a year's worth. I can't explain it, but I talked to the engineers, and they all said they have copies of their emails on their own systems and don't need the backups. So, it looks like there was no harm done, but I still can't explain it."

Gavin frowned and put the tips of his fingers together. "As long as no harm was done, I guess it's all right, especially since the employees have their own copies. You know what a stickler I am for doing everything by the book, and we're supposed to retain emails for a two-year period. You're sure there's no way to recover them?"

Should I tell him the whole story? "No. That's our only backup server. They're gone for good."

Gavin's frown deepened, and he folded his hands. "Tell me something, Tommy. Do you think we need another system administrator? Someone to assist you?"

Perspiration formed on Tommy's upper lip. *Uh-oh. Here it comes. He's upset about the server, and he's going to hire somebody else to eventually replace me.* "No, sir. I have time to cover the sysadmin work and even support some of the research when needed. I'll let you know if I need help."

"All right," Gavin said as he went back to typing on his laptop. "Thanks, Tommy. You can go now."

Tommy pushed himself up out of the chair and lumbered out of the office, quietly closing the door behind him. *I wonder what I have to do to save my job.*

CHAPTER 7

A t five minutes to three o'clock on Tuesday, Kate stepped out of her car in the parking lot next to the Sunset Trail. Barkley bounded out behind her and trotted around the car a couple of times, waiting for his owner to start their usual routine. Kate looked at the entrance to the running trail, at the park bench and the fencepost.

Runners and cyclists streamed along the path in both directions, but no one was sitting on the bench, and there was nothing on the fence post. *Nice weather. Lots of people in the park today. Nothing unusual.* She closed her car door, locked it, and bent over to re-tie her running shoes.

When she stood up, she saw an elderly woman wearing a heavy coat, a wool scarf, and large sunglasses, slowly making her way up the trail, using a cane. Her gray hair protruded out from beneath a red knit cap. She shuffled up to the bench and sat down.

Kate checked her watch. Three o'clock on the dot. As she and Barkley walked toward the trail head, she eyed the woman carefully. *Could she be part of the mystery? No way. She looks like she's in her eighties. And destitute. She certainly couldn't afford to play games with a gold watch.*

Kate stopped next to the bench, began her usual warmup and stretch, and peered down the trail to see if a more likely suspect would appear.

The elderly woman looked up at her. "Good afternoon," she said in a husky voice. "You must be going for a run."

"Yes, I am," Kate said as she faced her new companion.

The papery skin on the woman's face was marked with deep creases around her mouth, and the gray hair sticking out from beneath her hat was coarse and dry. She raised one gloved hand and pointed toward the sky. "It's a nice day to be outside exercising, isn't it?" She switched her cane to the other hand. "I used to be a runner myself, but those days are long gone."

Kate felt a twinge of guilt. This was probably a lonely old lady looking for a little civil conversation to brighten her day. Maybe the watch episode wasn't worth pursuing. Maybe she was making too much of a fluke. Maybe she should take a few minutes to be nice to this stranger.

"Were you a competitive runner?" Kate asked as she stretched her arms over her head.

"Oh yes. Of course, back then there weren't as many opportunities for women in athletics as there are today. I had some pretty good experiences, but I'd rather hear about your training. It would mean a great deal to me if you would keep me company for a few minutes just until I catch my breath."

"All right," Kate said as she sat on the bench. "I'm Kathryn Frasier."

Barkley plopped on the ground between them and accepted the little head pats from his new acquaintance.

"Nice to meet you, Kathryn. I'm Mrs. Finta." She pulled her knit cap farther down over her ears. "Do you run here often?"

"I'm out here four or five days a week. I'm training for a marathon."

"A marathon? That sounds hard. It's over twenty-six miles, isn't it?"

"Twenty-six point two miles, to be exact, and the training is pretty intense. I signed up for the Vancouver Marathon which is just a few months away, so I'm committed to doing it."

"I envy you. When I was young, women weren't allowed to run marathons. It must be wonderful to take on a challenge like that. Tell me, why did you decide to run a marathon?"

"Well, my parents died several months ago in a car accident, and my minister suggested I find something to focus on so I wouldn't spend so much time dwelling on the sadness. He and his wife thought training for a marathon would strengthen me mentally, physically, and spiritually."

"I'm sorry to hear about your loss," Mrs. Finta said as she leaned her cane against the bench and folded her hands in her lap, "but I think your minister had a good idea. I'm sure your parents would be very proud of you."

Their conversation turned to the benefits of aerobic exercise. They shared opinions on the joys of living in Bellevue. And the blessings of good parents.

I can't believe I'm pouring my heart and soul out to a little old lady I've never seen before, thought Kate. As if I've known her all my life.

Suddenly Barkley jumped up and darted across the trail to the edge of the lake, yapping at a formation of geese that had landed in the water. As the little dog pranced back and forth along the bank, announcing his displeasure with the intruders, the largest goose swam toward him, honking and flapping its wings aggressively. Barkley bolted back across the trail and scooted under the park bench.

Mrs. Finta tilted her head back, laughing and clapping her hands together.

Kate felt a spooky chill run up her spine. *The way she tilted her head and clapped her hands. I've seen my mother do that exact thing a thousand times.*

She looked away. *Get a grip on yourself. Lots of people laugh and clap their hands. Remember, we live in a rational world.*

Mrs. Finta managed to coax a chastened Barkley out from under the bench. "Don't worry, little one. Life is full of surprises, but things usually aren't as bad as they seem." She stroked the fur on his back until he stopped shaking, then she turned to Kate. "It's getting late. I'm sure you want to get on with your run, and I must be going." She pulled back a frayed sleeve on her coat and looked at her watch. "Goodness, it's later than I thought."

Kate gasped. *Are those diamonds around a rectangular face?* "Excuse me, but that looks just like a watch I found on the fencepost yesterday."

"So, you're the person who turned it in to the visitor's center?"

"Yes, I took it over there yesterday afternoon."

"Thank you for being so honest. This watch is very special to me."

"Then you must be Cece."

"That's right, I am," she said as she stood. "But I really must be going. I'm late for an appointment." She started to walk away.

Kate jumped up from the bench. "Wait. I want to talk to you about the watch."

Mrs. Finta looked back and smiled sweetly. "I'm sorry. I don't have time to talk to you now but thank you for a lovely afternoon. I promise we'll meet again soon, very soon, and I'll tell you the story behind the watch." She shook her head and exclaimed, "What a coincidence that we've met."

Kate stood frozen in amazement as the old woman walked to the parking lot, got in a car, and drove away.

What a coincidence? There are no coincidences.

CHAPTER 8

Of the many restaurants in Bellevue—and there are many, many restaurants in Bellevue—The Embers was Kate's favorite, though she rarely had the opportunity to dine at the five-star establishment. She wished Mr. Kaplan had given her a hint of why he wanted her to meet his clients at such a fancy place.

She arrived promptly at eight o'clock and asked for the Kaplan reservation. A hostess escorted her through the mahogany-paneled dining area to a large, private room at the back of the restaurant.

A fire crackled in the ornate fireplace at the far end of the room. Two small couches framed the area around the hearth with several chairs and a coffee table in front. A round dining table occupied the center of the room under the soft glow of a chandelier.

A man and woman sat next to each other on one of the couches. When they saw Kate, they rose and walked over to her. The woman spoke first. "Kathryn, thank you so much for coming."

Kate judged the woman to be in her sixties. Short, a little overweight, but stylish in a black suit with a red floral scarf around her neck. The overall impression was simple but expensive.

"I'm Sylvia Goldman, and this is my husband, Harry. Your mother was a close friend of mine in college."

A friend of mother's? Mr. Kaplan hadn't mentioned that.

Harry reached out from behind his wife to shake hands. Kate judged him to be about the same age as Sylvia. He was a tall man, almost a head taller than Sylvia, and heavily built, with a kindly face. He leaned slightly over his wife, as if to provide some protection for her. "We were so sorry to hear about your parents. Please accept our condolences."

They know about the accident?

Kate was sure she had never heard their names or seen these people before. She managed a polite "thank you" in response and decided her best course of action would be to say very little and wait to hear what this was all about. Were they here just to pay their respects? But where was Mr. Kaplan?

Sylvia seemed to anticipate her thought. "John Kaplan called to say he would be a few minutes late. Won't you come sit with us while we wait and have a glass of wine? It's very good pinot noir."

Kate followed the couple to the fireplace and took a seat in one of the chairs, but she declined the wine. As her eyes adjusted to the semi-dark room, Kate glanced around. The dining table was covered with an immaculate white tablecloth and surrounded by five plush chairs. *Mr. Kaplan must be bringing someone else with him.*

As Harry refreshed the wine in his wife's glass, the hostess escorted the fourth member of the group into the room. Even in the dim light, Kate immediately made out the sturdy round figure of John Kaplan, still dressed in a dark business suit from the day's work.

Kaplan was not a tall man. He was wide, but not fat, with a barrel chest that produced a resonant, confident voice. He had a large round head that was inhabited by a large, keen brain, and his dark eyes were clear and inquisitive behind rimless glasses. He was well-known in legal circles for his expertise in the law, and his overall demeanor was that of a self-assured lawyer who was accustomed to winning his cases and having his way. He had been the Frasiers' attorney for as long as Kate could remember. He immediately made his way over to her and took both of her hands in his.

"Hello, Kathryn. I'm so glad you could come tonight. I see you've already met the Goldmans." He addressed Sylvia and

Harry by their first names and shook hands with each of them. "Thank you for your patience. I was unexpectedly delayed with a new case."

Mr. Kaplan accepted a glass of wine from Harry and walked around in front of the fireplace to face the little group. "Knowing you all as well as I do," he said, "I took the liberty of ordering the ginger-encrusted salmon for everyone. It's the house special-ty and it's excellent. As soon as Cece arrives, we'll get down to business."

Cece? The old woman from the park? How does Mr. Kaplan know her?

Sylvia responded. "She should be here shortly." She leaned to-ward Kate and spoke quietly, as if confiding in her. "You'll have to forgive Cece. She does like to make an entrance. She's an ac-tress, you know, and can sometimes be a little melodramatic."

"Do you know Cece?" Kate asked.

"Oh yes, dear. We know her very well. Cece is our daughter."

CHAPTER 9

Kate stifled her urge to laugh out loud at the notion that the elderly woman she had encountered in Campbell Park could be the Goldmans' daughter. Was this lady kidding her? She firmly fixed her eyes on Sylvia's. "Mrs. Goldman, we can't be talking about the same person. The woman who introduced herself to me as Cece could not possibly be your daughter. She was old, quite old. She's much older than you are."

Sylvia didn't seem surprised. She sat back with a knowing look on her face. "I understand your confusion, dear. Like I said, Cece is an actress. A very good actress too, if I do say so myself."

At that moment, the restaurant's hostess opened the door and escorted a young woman into the room. The newcomer was dressed in a navy-blue silk blouse and slacks. She wore a simple strand of pearls around her neck, small pearl earrings, and a gold watch on her wrist. *The* gold watch!

As the newcomer approached the little group, the Goldmans stood and both of them gave her a hug. Sylvia said, "Kathryn, this is our daughter, Cece Goldman. Cece, meet Kathryn Frasier."

Kate stared in bewilderment. This certainly could not be the old lady she had met in Campbell Park. But it wasn't just the watch or the woman's age that left Kate gaping. It was simply the fact that this petite girl with bright blue eyes and lively blonde hair bore a startling resemblance to Kate's own mother.

Cece's face registered the self-satisfaction of having delivered a convincing performance in the park, but her expression was sincere, even courteous, as she stood in front of Kathryn. "I know this must be puzzling," she said, "but we'll explain everything over dinner."

Kate still didn't understand. "But if you're Cece, who was the woman I met in the park today?"

"Oh, that." Cece took a red knit cap out of her handbag and pulled it on. The gray wig sewn to the underside of the cap stuck out around the edges. "You can create just about any illusion you want with a little theatrical makeup and clothing. I'm glad it was so convincing, though. Gives me confidence in my acting ability."

Kate looked to Mr. Kaplan for help. "I don't understand."

John Kaplan placed his wine glass on the mantle. "Kathryn, I know you must be confused by all of this, and we owe you an explanation. Please, won't you all be seated?" He took one of the fireplace irons and poked at the fire while Sylvia and Harry returned to the couch. Kate and Cece sat side by side in two of the chairs.

"The Goldmans are old friends of mine. I've known them longer than I knew your parents. Harry was a classmate of mine in law school. Although we both passed the bar exam, he was more intelligent because he went back to Denver to start a jewelry business. It was a clever and lucrative decision on his part," he said as he winked at Harry. "His bracelets and trinkets don't complain about his ability to represent them." The Goldmans laughed along with Kaplan.

Harry said, "I would never have made the legal scholar John did. I was lucky to have something to fall back on."

"Nonsense," said Kaplan. He turned to Kate again. "Harry and Sylvia contacted me a week or so ago about a serious matter that concerns you, and we all felt it would be best to meet as a group."

Kate felt a chill go through her. As nice as they were, these people were strangers to her. What possible bearing could they have on her life? "What serious matter?" she asked.

Kaplan replaced the poker with the other fireplace implements. "Kathryn, we all know the grief you've suffered these last few months, and we certainly wouldn't want to do anything to disrespect you in this time of mourning for your parents. I wasn't sure if we should bring this information to you now, but I spoke with Reverend Whitefield, and he felt confident that you would want to know."

Kate felt another chill. *He spoke to my minister? Reverend Whitefield didn't say anything to me about that.* "I appreciate your concern for me. Please tell me what this is all about."

Kaplan continued, "Sylvia is going to tell you some history about your family you probably don't know. Sylvia?"

Sylvia's face was full of genuine compassion as she looked into Kate's eyes. She cleared her throat, took a sip of wine, and put her glass on the table.

"Kathryn, you remember I told you that your mother and I were good friends in college. We were both history majors and had several classes together. We were quite different people. I was a good bit older than the other girls because it had taken me a long time to save up enough to go to college. I was bookish and had to study hard to get good grades, while Leah was outgoing and naturally bright. She was beautiful and popular, while I was more of an ugly duckling."

Harry interrupted. "You were never an ugly duckling, Sylvia."

Sylvia smiled, patted his hand, and continued. "As I said, we were quite different personalities, but we became good friends. We had a lot in common. We both wanted to make a positive impact, to make the world a better place.

"After we graduated, we went separate ways. I had met Harry in my senior year, and he and I married shortly after graduation and moved to Denver where Harry started his jewelry business. At the same time, your mother had taken a job as a secretary in a small business firm.

"I received a letter from her a year or so after graduation. She said she was bored with her secretarial job but had recently joined a political campaign as a volunteer. She was almost effervescent in her enthusiasm for this new cause. The politician was a young man who was running for state assemblyman, his first political campaign, and I gathered that he was as eager to improve people's lives as she was to help him do it."

Mother worked on a political campaign? thought Kate. *She never mentioned that to me. As a matter of fact, she always said she hated politics.*

A waitress entered with their dinners, and everyone moved to the dining table. They settled into their chairs, adjusted napkins and waited as the dinners were set before them. Cece sat just to Kate's left and Sylvia to her right. Harry was next to Sylvia, and Mr. Kaplan occupied the remaining seat. A steward poured wine for each of them, checked that they had everything they wanted, and left the room. The five diners were alone.

Kaplan suggested they enjoy their dinners before continuing Sylvia's narrative. As they sampled their meals with quiet comments of approval, Kate shifted in her chair, wondering to herself. *Why are they telling me all this stuff about my mother's life? Is this some kind of trip down memory lane that I'm supposed to be enjoying?*

CHAPTER 10

K ate picked at her food, trying to imagine where the story was going.

As they were nearing the end of the meal, Mr. Kaplan suggested that Sylvia continue the narrative.

Sylvia folded and refolded the napkin in her lap. She took a last bite of salmon, chewed slowly, and looked to her husband as if seeking reassurance. Harry nodded his encouragement. She took a deep breath and turned toward Kate.

"The next part of the story will be difficult for me to tell, Kathryn, and it will be hard for you to hear. I'm telling you this because we believe it is your right to know. Do I have your permission to continue?"

Kate's chest tightened. *Hard for me to hear? What can this be?* She sat straight up in her chair, took a drink of water, and determined to remain calm no matter what this was. She looked around the table and saw four pairs of eyes gazing at her in candid concern. "Please go on."

"Several months after I received the letter from your mother, she called me. She said she had a difficult decision to make and wanted to know if I would help. Of course, I said yes, and she asked if she could visit us. Harry had been successful in his business, and we were fortunate to have moved into a modest home. We were delighted to have her come.

"When your mother arrived, she was obviously in great distress. The day she came to our house, she and I sat and talked for several hours about her situation. Apparently, she and the young politician on whose campaign she was working had grown very close. I guess you could even say she had fallen in love."

Sylvia's voice became very soft and measured. "Your mother was pregnant."

* * *

Kate shivered. "This can't be true," she whispered.

Sylvia's eyes were wet with tears as she put her hand on Kate's. "I'm sorry, Kathryn, but I assure you it is true."

While Sylvia dabbed at her eyes with a handkerchief, Mr. Kaplan interjected, "That was in 1980. You have to understand the sensitivity back then to an issue like this. It could have caused a scandal that would have been fatal to the politician's future."

1980? That was several years before I was born. Mother was pregnant with another child?

Sylvia continued, "He told her that he had no intention of marrying her and she should have an abortion. Your mother refused. He said that he would not allow her to ruin his promising career and insisted she have an abortion in secret. She was frightened, not sure how far he would go, so she agreed to his demand. She told him she was going to another state to see friends who would help her arrange the abortion, and that's when she came to us."

"My mother would never have agreed to an abortion."

"You're right," Sylvia said. "Leah was adamant that she would not abort the child, but she didn't know how she could care for a baby, given her financial and marital situation. Somewhere during the days of introspection and prayer, the idea of adoption came up. It was as if our three minds had all fashioned the same idea at the same time. You see, Harry and I had been told by doctors that we couldn't have children. A month or so before the due date, Leah asked if we would adopt the baby. We were both thrilled and devastated at the same time. I want you to know that the decision came completely from your mother and grew out of an intense and fervent love for the child."

Sylvia paused again as the four people around the table waited for a response. Kate slowly shifted her gaze away from Sylvia and looked at Cece. If this story was true, Kate realized she was looking into the face of her older half-sister. Cece's clear blue eyes all but verified the story. *Just like Mother's eyes. And the way she tilted her head back and laughed today in the park. It's true. It's unbelievable, but it's true.*

Mr. Kaplan reached into his jacket pocket and took out an envelope. "This is where I come into the story, Kathryn. Harry and Sylvia asked me to make the arrangements, and we were able to secure the adoption. I have the papers here." He handed the envelope to Kate. It contained a birth certificate for Cecelia Leah Dawson. Born to Leah Dawson, March 14, 1980. The father's name was not listed. A second document was the amended certificate changing the baby's last name to Goldman and listing the adoptive parents as Sylvia and Harry Goldman.

"Did my father know about this?"

Sylvia answered. "Your parents met a couple of years later, and Leah told him the story of Cece before they married."

"But why didn't they tell me about this themselves?"

Once again Sylvia placed her hand on Kate's, like a mother comforting a beloved child. "We know from meeting with them after you were born that they agonized over whether or not they should share this information with you when you were old enough to understand it. Several years ago, Leah told me that she desperately wanted to tell you. Since you were their only child and your parents had no siblings, she wanted you to know you had a sister in the world, but she kept putting it off because she was afraid. Your mother was a good woman, a good wife and mother. She couldn't bear the thought of hurting you or harming the wonderful family relationship you all shared."

Kate paused for a few seconds, letting it sink in. Her eyes were locked on Sylvia's. "But why are you telling me this now? You could have kept it a secret, and I never would have known."

Harry interceded and gestured toward his adopted daughter. "Cece has been aware of the story of her birth for a long time. Even though you didn't know about her, she has known about you. We wouldn't have brought this information to you if either of your parents were alive. But after we learned of your parents' deaths and knowing that your mother wanted to eventually share this secret with you, Cece insisted we talk to you."

Cece leaned toward Kate. "You're my closest blood relative, and I wanted us to get to know each other and develop the kind of relationship that only sisters can have."

There was an awkward silence. Then Kate reached over and hesitantly took the hand of her older half-sister, and Cece clasped her hand within her two. Both girls' faces were wet with tears.

CHAPTER 11

K ate wiped the tears out of her eyes and took a long swallow of water. Then she asked about her parents' relationship with the Goldmans after Cece was born.

Sylvia explained. "Your parents felt they shouldn't interfere with Cece's upbringing, so they never came to see us. However, Leah and I kept in touch through letters and emails."

Kate turned back to Cece, who was still holding her hand. "When did you learn all of this?"

"My parents told me I was adopted when I was a young child, but I didn't know who my biological mother was until I was eighteen. That's when Mom and Dad gave me the watch that Leah wanted me to have." She held up her left wrist. "The watch you found on the fencepost."

"Why set up the elaborate meeting in the park in disguise? Why not just be yourself?"

"I had a couple of reasons. First, I wanted to meet you before we revealed the information about your mother's background. We knew this was going to be a shock no matter how we presented it to you. If I had sensed that you were too vulnerable to handle it, we wouldn't have told you. You convinced me during our conversation that you wouldn't hide from the truth, no matter where it took you."

"And your second reason?"

"I wanted to get an idea of who you really are. You can tell a lot about somebody by the way they treat the poor and the elderly, so I disguised myself as a poor old lady to see how you would react. You showed me such kindness and respect as we sat on the park bench that I felt a sense of sisterhood with you immediately." She gently squeezed Kate's hand.

"But you told me your name was Mrs. Finta."

"That was a bit of artful dodging." Cece looked quite pleased with herself. "Cecelia Finta is my stage name. *Finta* is Italian for 'pretense.'"

Kate looked in admiration at her sister. "Your mother is right. You really are a good actress. You completely fooled me."

As the meeting broke up, Mr. Kaplan said, "Kathryn, could you meet us in my office tomorrow at ten? There are a few more details I'd like to discuss with you."

"Yes, certainly. Ten o'clock is fine."

As Kate drove home, she felt a surprising sense of completion, as if someone had given her the final piece to a puzzle—a piece she didn't even know was missing. The thought of having an older half-sister was less of a shock than it should have been. It felt right, and she wondered why. *Was there some clue in my parents' behavior over the years that hinted at Cece's existence? Did they have conversations when I was a baby that are somehow buried deep in my subconscious? Or is there some outside force in the universe so strong that it informs your soul even when there's no earthly explanation?*

But why did Mr. Kaplan set up another meeting for tomorrow? A few miles short of her house, a thought came to her that made her nearly veer off the road. Did her half-sister want a share of the inheritance?

* * *

Kate took the old photo album down from its place, sat on the couch, and with Barkley nestled beside her, opened it to the picture of her mother wearing the watch.

Her mother's smile brought back tender memories. Like when she was in preschool and her mother took her to the library every week, holding her hand and chatting about all the wonderful things they were going to read. Even today, she could recall the musty smell of the library books mingled with the lavender fragrance of her mother's cologne.

And sitting at the kitchen table when she was seven or eight years old, reading riddles out of a child's joke book while her mother made dinner and pretended not to know the answers until Kate read them out.

And as a teenager, being cajoled into the semi-annual chore of what her mother playfully called "the dreaded shopping spree," a reference to Kate's disinterest in her wardrobe and dislike of having to spend time buying clothes. The result was a compromise between comfort for Kate and fashion for Leah, always followed by a celebration of their success over an ice cream sundae.

Gazing at the old picture now, Kate felt the weight of her privilege. "It's okay, Mother," she said out loud. Tears dropped onto the plastic cover that protected the picture. "I know about Cece, and it's all right."

Holding the photo album in her lap, Kate fell asleep on the couch. She dreamt that she was walking along a trail in Campbell Park, and there were open fields all around. A single large oak tree stood next to the trail, and a white bird sat on a branch of the tree. Suddenly, a man and a woman appeared walking toward her, hand in hand. Her father and mother. As they got close, Kate's mother took off the gold watch she was wearing and held it out to her. "With time all things are revealed," she said.

As Kate reached for the watch, the white bird flew down from the tree and landed on her father's shoulder.

CHAPTER 12

Wednesday

Kate arrived at Mr. Kaplan's office at ten o'clock on Wednesday and found the Goldmans already there. She sensed that she had interrupted a solemn conversation.

Mr. Kaplan rose from behind his enormous mahogany desk to greet her, and then each of the Goldmans welcomed her.

Sylvia wanted to know if she had slept well.

"Thanks for your concern, Mrs. Goldman. To be honest, I did lie awake for a while, but I got enough sleep, and I'm anxious to learn what this meeting is all about."

Harry shook hands with her; Cece approached and the two girls delicately, but warmly, embraced each other.

Kaplan leaned against his desk, asked the others to be seated, and began the meeting without any small talk. "Kathryn, let me get right to the point. We want to talk to you about your parents' automobile accident."

"Mr. Kaplan, I don't like to talk about the accident or even think about it."

"I understand. But the Goldmans have shared some things with me about the accident that you may not know."

Kate looked in surprise at Harry and Sylvia. How could they know more about that awful incident than she did? "I read the complete police report," she said. "I can't imagine there's anything about the accident that I don't know."

Kaplan picked up a copy of the report from his desk. "Yes, I saw the police report also." He flipped to the last page. "They concluded that your parents' car had accidentally driven off the side of the mountain road and was destroyed in the subsequent explosion and fire, which also took your parents' lives. But the Goldmans have produced some information that wasn't considered at the time because no one was aware of it."

Kate frowned and sat up straighter in her chair. "What information?"

Sylvia reached into her purse and took out her phone. "Your mother sent me an email a week or so before the accident saying she and your father were going on vacation to Reno, Nevada, and would be attending a performance of the Western Ballet Company. You know your mother was such a fan of the ballet."

"Yes, I remember," Kate said. "They were going to a matinee performance of *Giselle*. It was one of mother's favorites."

Sylvia typed her password into the screen on her phone. "I had asked her to let me know her opinion of the ballet company's performance since they were scheduled to tour through Denver, and I would have loved to see *Giselle* again.

"Your mother mentioned in that particular email that she was glad the theater was close to the hotel so they could walk to the theater without ever having to drive through the mountains. I remembered that your mother was quite afraid of heights, especially driving on mountain roads."

Kate nodded. "That's right. Dad used to call her his 'valley girl' because she had an irrational fear of driving on mountain roads. She would never let him go near one. I was shocked when I learned how the accident happened. They must have somehow ended up on that mountain road by mistake."

Harry leaned forward in his chair with his forearms on his legs. "That's what we thought, too, when we heard about it. But then Sylvia remembered something that caused us grave concern and made it essential that we contact you."

Sylvia tapped the screen on her cell phone a couple of times. "I remembered I had received an email from your mother on the day of the accident. I have it here on my phone. Let me show you."

Sylvia handed the phone over, and Kate stared at the last email her mother had sent.

"Dear Sylvia, I hope this email finds you and your family well. We had a pleasant flight to Reno and have enjoyed our time here so far. Unfortunately, I won't be able to give you my opinion on the performance of *Giselle* after all. An acquaintance of Bill's has asked us to join him for an early dinner tonight, so we had to exchange our tickets from the matinee to the evening performance, which is a different ballet. Bill is being very mysterious about this, but he tells me this meeting will result in extremely good news. All the best, Leah."

Kate handed Sylvia's phone back to her. "So, they didn't attend the matinee performance after all?" She tried to reconstruct the events of the day her parents died. "The accident happened around seven-thirty. If they had tickets for an evening performance, they wouldn't have been on the road then. Maybe their plans for an early dinner fell through."

"That could be," said Harry, "but considering the unusual circumstances, the sudden change in plans, the mysterious meeting with an unnamed acquaintance, and your mother's fear of driving on mountain roads, it seemed to us like there may have been foul play. Or at least someone should look at the possibility of it."

Kate felt her mouth go dry. "Foul play?" She shook her head vigorously. "That's impossible. My parents didn't have any enemies. Why didn't you contact the authorities if you suspected foul play?"

Kaplan put the police report back on his desk. "The Goldmans contacted me, asking if there should be an investigation. But all of this is just circumstantial evidence, nothing the police could use as a basis for an investigation. We need to have something more concrete before we contact the authorities. We were hoping you might remember something."

Kate stood and paced behind her chair, searching her memory. "No, I can't think of anything that would support this idea."

"Did your parents ever mention any problems with other people, bad feelings, professional jealousies?" Kaplan asked.

"No, nothing I can think of."

"Did they say anything to you about meeting a friend for dinner the day they died? Do you know who it might have been?"

"No. I hadn't heard from them since they left for their vacation. I had no idea they were meeting anyone in Reno."

"Did you notice any odd behavior by your parents before they left for their trip? Were either of them acting out of character?"

Kate put her hands on the back of the chair and shook her head slowly. "No, I didn't notice anything unusual."

"What about their belongings they took with them to Reno. Did you find anything strange or odd in their suitcases?"

Kate sighed. "I don't know. The hotel people packed up their belongings into their suitcases and shipped them to me. I haven't had the heart to go through them. They're still in the guest room closet at my house."

Kaplan walked back behind his desk and took a seat. "We may be chasing the wind," he said, "but it would be wise to examine every detail just so we can put our own minds to rest. I think it would be a way to honor your parents. Of course, the decision is yours on whether or not to proceed. Take whatever time you need to think about it."

"I don't need any time to think about it. If there's some doubt about the accident, we should definitely try to find the truth. I'll go home and look through the suitcases to see if there's anything there." Kate felt her mind shift to another gear. Finally, here was something productive she could do. "Cece, would you like to come over and help me? We can eat something for lunch and then go through the suitcases."

"Yes. I can drop Mom and Dad off at their place and pick up a pizza and come right over."

Kate gave her the address and directions. "Great. I'll see you in an hour."

Sylvia took both of Kate's hands in hers. "Kathryn, would you like to join us for Shabbat dinner on Friday? We're renting an apartment here, and we would love to spend the evening with you."

"I'd like that, Mrs. Goldman. Thanks for asking."

"We look forward to having you over, dear. It seems we always receive a blessing on the Sabbath."

CHAPTER 13

A little after noon, Cece arrived at Kate's home with the pizza. Barkley trotted up to her and cocked his head to one side, trying to reconcile her smell with the way she looked now.

"It's just a plain cheese pizza," Cece said as she followed Kate into the kitchen and laid the box on the table. "Hope that's okay with you."

Kate put plates and silverware on the table. She looked up and grinned. "Perfect. That's exactly the way I like it best."

Cece clapped her hands together. "Me too. I'm glad to know we have something in common. I mean, we're sisters, but we don't look anything alike. You're a tall brunette with straight hair and brown eyes. I'm short with curly blonde hair and blue eyes." She ruffled her own locks. "Not much in common there."

Kate pulled a chair out for her sister. "Have a seat, and we'll start eating the first thing we have in common," she said with a chuckle.

After they finished lunch, the two girls and the little collie moved into the living room. Kate led Cece over to the bookshelves and pointed out some of the photos of her with her parents. She took the old album down and showed Cece the picture where she had first identified the gold watch.

They sat on the couch as Cece leafed through the pages. "Tell me about your parents," she said. "I'd like to know what they were like."

Kate settled back and hugged her knees to her chest. "My father was an electrical engineer, incredibly intelligent and very much the absent-minded professor type." She laughed when she related how he couldn't remember his phone number and would occasionally get lost when driving even close to home. "He was a wonderful person and a devoted family man. He gave me my love of puzzles and math problems."

"Ah! That explains all the crossword puzzles on your coffee table."

"Yeah. We would play games for hours. Mother called us 'fraternal twins born thirty years apart.' "

"It's nice to have so much in common with your parents."

"Dad also loved wordplay. Some of his puns were clever and funny, but others were so bad that Mother and I would just groan at them. But Dad never cared. No matter how good or bad they were, he always took great delight in them." She sighed. "I miss him so much, but I guess you'd rather know more about mother."

"Yes, I would. Tell me about her."

Kate pointed to the last picture in the album. "You can see from the photo that you look quite a bit like her when she was young. You seem to have her personality too. You see, Dad and I were quiet and introverted, but Mother was vivacious and energetic. She was always in a good mood, always smiling. I remember waking up in the mornings and hearing her singing while she made breakfast."

"That's interesting, because I like to sing when I get out of bed in the morning."

Kate considered her next comments carefully. "I always thought of Mother as the kind of woman I wanted to be. She was graceful and self-assured while I was shy and awkward. It's not unusual for me to trip over the corner of a rug or bump my knee into the edge of a coffee table. She always looked beautiful and neat while I was usually a mess. Last night when I learned about my mother's past, I think I saw her as a real person for the first time, instead of the perfect icon I had created in my mind." Kate's voice grew softer. "It must have been so hard for her to keep this bottled up inside all those years."

The two girls sat quietly for a minute. Finally, Kate put the photo album back on the shelf and said, "I've been thinking about our meeting this morning. I can't believe there could have been any foul play involved. But I'm ready to look into every detail that's available to me to uncover the truth about what happened that night."

Cece patted Barkley's head as she talked. "Did your father carry a cell phone or a laptop? Anything that might provide a clue to their whereabouts while they were in Reno?"

"He didn't own a cell phone. He said he knew he'd just lose it. But he always took his laptop with him on trips. The charred remains of it were found at the site of the crash. There's no way to get any information off of it."

"How about your mother?"

"Her cell phone was also found at the crash site. It was completely burned up. She didn't have a laptop."

Cece scratched her head. "The real mysterious part of this is the person they met for dinner. Do you know who it might have been?"

"No idea at all. Mother's email doesn't give any clue except that it was somebody that my dad knew." Kate walked over to the mantle and adjusted a couple of candlesticks. She shook her head slowly. "I don't know where to go from here."

Cece joined her at the fireplace and faced her sister. "Why don't we start by looking at the original source of the problem: the politician who caused your mother—I mean, our mother—such anguish to begin with. Could he have been involved?"

Kate stopped positioning the candlesticks and looked skeptically at Cece. "Why would he pop up so many years after the fact? It's been decades since he was involved. Besides, we don't even know who he is."

Cece blushed and looked at her feet. "I know who he is."

Kate's eyes opened wide in anticipation. "You know?"

"Yes. Do you want me to tell you?"

"Of course. I have to know."
"My mom told me. It's Representative Robert Hodges."

CHAPTER 14

Kate's mouth dropped open. "Robert Hodges? My mother with Robert Hodges?" she cried. "He's running for governor right now! He's the jerk who did that to my mother?"

An expression of sadness crossed Cece's face, and she blushed even deeper.

Kate immediately realized her mistake. "Oh, Cece, I'm so sorry. He's your biological father, and I had no business calling him a jerk. Please forgive me."

"There's nothing to forgive. I actually agree with you."

"But why would he want to get back into the picture now?"

"I don't know, but some politicians will go to any length to protect their careers. Maybe something came up that brought back his old scandal. Is there any way we can get information about him?"

Kate walked back to the couch, sat down and shook her head. "I don't know many people who are involved in politics." All of a sudden, she sat up straight and snapped her fingers. "Wait a minute. A friend of mine told me he was volunteering with the Hodges campaign. I'll call him. Maybe we can learn something. If I get a chance to meet Hodges, do you want to come with me?"

"I'd be okay with meeting your friend, but I don't want to get anywhere near Robert Hodges. First of all, I don't think I'm emotionally prepared for it. Also, if he takes one look at me, he might guess that I'm Leah's daughter. If he has anything to do with this, we don't want to play that card."

"Good point. Let me call now and see if we can set something up."

When she reached Tommy Abrahams on the phone, Kate told him she wanted to bring a friend by the office to meet him.

"You wouldn't be trying to set me up with someone, now would you, Kate?" he teased.

She laughed. "No. We've been thinking about volunteering for the Hodges campaign, though, and I remember you talking about it. Any chance you could arrange for us to meet him?"

"Great timing, Kathryn. Hodges will be in town tomorrow, and he's supposed to be at campaign headquarters in the afternoon. Why don't you come to my office around one o'clock, and we'll walk over together."

"Sounds good. Thanks, Tommy."

She clicked off her phone and gave Cece a thumbs-up. "We're all set for tomorrow. We'll meet Tommy at ArcTron Labs at one o'clock. If we drive separately, you can take off when he and I go to the campaign headquarters."

Cece had been pacing around the room while Kate talked to Tommy. Now she stopped and planted her hands on her hips. "I want to know what you honestly think of Hodges. And promise you won't sugarcoat it for me."

"I promise. If I meet him, I'll let you know everything."

Kate stood up. "Now that the meeting with Hodges is settled, I guess we need to move on to the real reason you're here. I've put off going through the suitcases long enough. Are you ready?"

"If you are."

CHAPTER 15

Kate led Cece to the guest room. After taking a deep breath, she opened the closet door and moved the shoeboxes she'd stacked in front. She pulled out the larger of the two suitcases and heaved it onto the bed. Biting her bottom lip, Kate opened it.

Piece by piece, she removed the clothes, jewelry, and toiletries and laid them next to the suitcase. Her mom's long black dress still held a hint of her favorite lavender fragrance.

"It's okay to cry," Cece said softly.

Kate looked at her sister. "No. The time for crying is past. Now we're going to figure out what happened to my parents."

They unzipped a side pocket and found tickets for the ballet's evening performance. "I guess they did exchange the matinee tickets," Kate noted. "But these tickets haven't been torn. They never made it to the theater."

Cece took the tickets and looked at them. "They must have left their dinner meeting late and decided to drive rather than walk."

"But my father would never have driven on those mountain roads on purpose. He would have known how frightened Mother would be. They must have made a wrong turn somewhere. It's the only thing that makes any sense."

"Maybe there's something in your father's suitcase."

They pulled the other suitcase out. In addition to the clothes and shoes, they found a shaving kit. Inside the kit was a yellow Post-it note: "Remind K to take her car to the shop."

"Did your father always remind you to take your car in for a checkup?" Cece asked.

"No, not at all. I have an old Nissan Maxima, and I always take it in on my birthday month and six months later for maintenance.

He never reminded me before, but my birthday was coming up."
Kate grimaced.

"Did you make the appointment?"

"No. My life went on hold after the accident. Actually, I have an appointment to take my car in tomorrow morning. I hate going there, though. It means I have to talk to Phil Warren, and he always treats me like I have the plague."

"Who is Phil Warren? And why would you keep going there if you don't like him?"

"Phil owns the auto repair shop and was a friend of my father's. My folks always took their cars to him, and my dad wanted me to do the same. But Phil Warren seems to really dislike me."

"How could anybody dislike you?"

Kate moved the suitcase out of the way and sat down on the side of the bed. "I don't know. I try to be nice. The first time I took my car there was right after I moved back to Bellevue after college. I've always been shy around handsome men, and he is really gorgeous—tall, blond hair, blue eyes, a great build."

Cece giggled. "Sounds like you've been paying attention, sister."

Kate blushed. "Everybody pays attention to Phil Warren. They say most of the women in Bellevue take their cars to his shop just because of him."

Cece sat down on a chair facing Kate. "So, he's a ladies' man?"

"No, not at all. My dad told me how incredibly serious and smart he is, and how he dropped out of a prestigious university to return home and take care of his mother and sister after his father died."

"Something like that takes a lot of character."

"Yeah. I was so intimidated on that first meeting that I tried to be very businesslike so he wouldn't think of me as a stupid college girl, but he just brushed me off like an insect. Now when I take my car in, I'm so nervous I just clam up. And he always goes through the same old routine." She put a mock frown on her face and deepened her voice to make it sound manly. "Hello, Miss Frasier. How's the Maxima? Give me your keys. Good-bye."

"He calls you Miss Frasier?"

"Yes. Never 'Kathryn.' Always 'Miss Frasier.' "

"Maybe it's his age. Is he a lot older than you?"

"No. I think he's around thirty years old."

Music came from Cece's purse. "Oops, that's my alarm. I had a feeling I'd lose track of the time once we started talking. I have to run some errands for my folks." She grabbed her phone and tapped the screen. "Good luck with your car guy. I'll talk to you tomorrow."

After Cece left, Kate stared at the little note her dad had scribbled and thought about her past encounters with Phil Warren. *Sure, it took a lot of character to give up the promise of a great career and do what he had to in order to overcome his father's bankruptcy and death. They say he even paid back all his father's creditors. But did he have to be so rude?*

"He'd make a good son-in-law," Kate's dad had told her on several occasions. "And it'd be great to have an auto mechanic in the family. Think of the savings!" Her mother had supported his case. "The two of you would look so nice together."

Of course, her parents had teased her about any single man she came in contact with. When she'd dated a lawyer a couple of years earlier, they sang the same melody but with different lyrics. "Free legal advice!" her father had said.

And there was the brilliant physics student when she was a senior in college. He was just a good friend, not a romantic interest, but her parents declared that it would be wonderful to have a genius in the family.

Kate knew it was all good-natured kidding, tinged with a little hope, but her father seemed to discover more positive attributes in Phil Warren than in any of the others.

Well, Dad, I'll tell you this. If there's one man on earth I can't imagine ever marrying, it's Phil Warren.

CHAPTER 16

Thursday

Phil Warren sat in his office Thursday morning and watched as Kathryn drove her car onto the lot. Nine forty-five. Just as punctual as Ben had predicted. *So, the princess has arrived.*

Five years ago, he had seen that same young woman step out of that same car for the first time. Her purse strap had caught in the car door, and it yanked her back when she started to move away. He had chuckled as he watched her disentangle herself from her automobile.

His first impression was that she was cute and genuine, and he wanted to meet her. He had asked one of the junior mechanics if he knew her.

"Yeah, that's Kathryn Frasier, Dr. Frasier's daughter. I was in high school with her. She and I weren't exactly in the same classes. She was one of the whiz kids, all A's and Advanced Placement courses. I remember her as being pretty nerdy and scrawny back then, but she sure isn't scrawny now, is she?"

Dr. Frasier had asked Phil to look out for her when she brought her car in, so he had walked over and politely introduced himself. "Hi. You must be Kathryn Frasier. I'm Phil Warren."

So much for first impressions. But that was then, and this is now. He smiled as he left his office to go out to the repair floor. *Guess what, princess? Things have changed.*

* * *

Kate got out of her car and saw Phil come onto the shop floor from the office area. Same variety of blue cotton shirt he always wore with the sleeves rolled up to the elbow and denim jeans. Always carrying a greasy cloth in his hands. She had a familiar giddy feeling as he walked toward her. But something was different today—he was smiling.

"Hello, Kathryn. How have you been?" He actually seemed interested.

He called me Kathryn? And smiled? That's a surprise. "I'm fine, thank you."

"How's the Maxima holding up?"

End of warm-hearted greeting. Back to the same old routine, she thought as she handed him the key to her car. "It's great. No problems at all. Just time for its checkup."

"Let's take a look."

The two walked over to her car, and he opened the driver's door. Phil and his mechanics always attached a small note to the door frame on the driver's side that contained information about the maintenance done on the car, including the mileage and date. As he slipped into the driver's seat, he leaned over to review the sticker from the last maintenance visit.

"That's strange," he said.

"What's strange?"

"There's another note attached here below mine." He turned his face up to look at her and gave a wry smile. "You haven't been unfaithful to me, have you, Kathryn? Did you take your car to another repair shop?"

Kate blushed. "Of course not." She knelt down beside him to get a better look at the note on the door frame. "What is it?"

"It's just a little piece of paper with some handwriting on it." Phil squinted to make out the writing. "It says, 'Behold the first day.' " He leaned closer and read it again. " 'Behold the first day.' That's what it says, all right. Do you know what it means?" This time his gaze lingered on her face while she considered the note.

"No. I don't have any idea. Do you suppose one of your mechanics put it there?"

"Not unless they want to get fired. I'd say you've got a practical joker on your hands." He raised his eyebrows and grinned. "Or maybe a boyfriend with a secret message?"

Is he flirting with me? she thought. *After five years of ignoring me? Impossible.* "Can you take it off the door? Can you get it off without tearing it?"

"I think so." Phil took a small tool out of his pocket and carefully scraped the note off the door frame. "There you go," he said as he gave it to Kate. She noticed the calluses on his hands. *A man who works with his hands. And based on his success, he works with his brain too.*

They both stood up. Kate held the little note in her hands, and Phil stood just behind her right shoulder, looking down at the paper. She could feel his breath on her neck, and her heart beat a little faster.

His voice was quiet and serious. "Do you have any idea what it means?"

"No, I don't understand it," she replied as matter-of-factly as she could. When she spun around to face him, she lost her balance, and he caught her by the shoulders to steady her. Their faces were just inches apart. "Oh dear," she said as she quickly stepped back and bumped into the side of her car. Phil looked down at her, tender amusement playing at the corners of his lips.

Is he laughing at me?

"Hey, Phil. I need your advice on this starter," one of his mechanics called out.

Without taking his eyes off Kate, he answered, "Be right there." He lowered his voice and addressed her again. "Look, we have a lot of cars in today, so we may have to keep yours for a few days. You can get a loaner from Maclean. I'll call you when your car is ready." He stood for a few seconds as if he was going to say something else, but then he just turned and walked away. Kate watched him go and felt a pleasurable uneasiness about their momentary encounter. *Did I really say "Oh dear?" That's the best I can come up with when I'm standing lip-to-lip with a handsome man? I'm hopeless!*

She put the tiny scrap of paper in her purse. As she walked toward the exit, she could still feel the imprint of his hands on her shoulders.

When she reached for the door handle, she glanced back and saw Phil gazing at her. He was leaning against a car with one hand on the fender and the other on his hip, and she suddenly wondered what it would feel like to have his arms around her. *Oh dear.*

When she got home, she took the little note out of her bag, laid it on the dining room table, and stared at it. She compared it with the one she and Cece had taken from her father's suitcase. The handwriting was small, but it was unmistakable. Her father had written this note and glued it to the door frame.

But why? When? And what did it mean? Could this be part of the puzzle?

After pacing back and forth in her living room for several minutes, she found her phone and called.

"Cece, can you come over to my place? I think I just got a piece of the puzzle."

CHAPTER 17

" 'Behold the first day.' What does that mean?" Cece wrinkled her forehead as she examined the tiny scrap of paper. Kate told her about the trip to the auto shop and the discovery of the note.

"I don't know," Kate replied, "but this is definitely my father's handwriting." She handed Cece the Post-it note they had found in her father's suitcase. "See, the writing is the same. That must have been why he wanted to remind me to have the car checked out. He knew I'd find this note. It's so typical of him. He's leaving a trail for me to follow, but it's all in code. We have to decipher the pieces to solve the puzzle."

Cece tilted her head to the side. "Do you think this could have something to do with the accident?"

Kate took the notes from Cece and laid them on the coffee table. "I don't know. My father used to do things like this to lead me to a birthday gift or a Christmas present. This could just be another one of those games. But if Dad had any idea that he or my mother were in danger, he might have left signs for me to follow. Maybe this will lead us to the answer."

"But how do you even start to figure it out?"

Kate picked up a puzzle book lying on the coffee table. "It's like one of these crosswords. The clues make sense, but not always in the way you typically think of them. It's the same with your disguises, Cece. People see something and understand it on the surface, but the reality may be different. We need to look at this from a fresh angle, to see it in another context." She laid the puzzle book back on the table. "What do you think 'the first day' could mean?"

"Could it be something like 'This is the first day of the rest of your life'?"

"Hmm." Kate chewed on her bottom lip while she thought. "Maybe."

"It could have something to do with Sunday. That's the first day of the week."

"Good point. It could mean Sunday. But I don't see why. We'll probably come up with more ideas if we just think about it awhile."

"Maybe you'll figure it out. I'm not sure I'll be much help with something like this."

"We'll figure it out together. In the meantime, let's grab a bite to eat before we head over to ArcTron Labs to meet Tommy."

Cece followed Kate into the kitchen. "Tell me about ArcTron Labs."

Kate talked while she smeared pimento cheese on wheat bread for their sandwiches. "ArcTron is this really great company. They hire engineers to invent and patent new electronics products, and they share the revenues with the employees. My dad couldn't refuse when they offered him a job there."

"Your dad worked there?"

"Yeah. He retired as a professor of electrical engineering at the university to work for ArcTron. My mom used to say the building should be glowing on the outside from all the brain power on the inside."

Cece took a bite of her sandwich. "Is it like Frankenstein's lab with lightning bolts flashing all over the place?" She made an ugly face and gestured wildly with her hands.

Kate laughed. "I haven't seen any monsters yet. But you never know what could come out of an electronics lab."

CHAPTER 18

K ate pulled into the rear parking lot while Cece followed in her own car. She hadn't been to ArcTron Labs since her father's death, and she took a deep breath as she got out of her car.

Kate and Cece entered the building and proceeded down the long hall that bisected the small, one-story structure. The north side of the building belonged to ArcTron; the south side had been rented to a customer service organization but lost its tenants when their jobs were moved overseas. It was currently vacant.

Halfway down the hall, they came to a set of double glass doors on the left with "ArcTron Labs" printed on them. Kate pressed the bell, the door buzzed, and they entered the lobby.

There was no receptionist, just a dozen chairs and some small tables. On the left side of the lobby was the door to the office of the CEO. On the right side was the entry to a hall that led to employees' offices and lab areas.

As Kate directed Cece toward Tommy's area on the right, the CEO's office door opened, and Gavin Connelly stepped out. Kate was pleased to see him. Although she didn't know Gavin well, she felt indebted to him for overseeing the company her father had loved so much. "Wait, Cece," she said. "I want you to meet someone."

As Gavin approached, she noticed dark circles under his eyes. *Probably working too hard and not getting enough sleep*, she thought. *So many engineers get lost in their jobs and don't take care of themselves, especially the single ones.*

Gavin extended his hand. "Kathryn, I didn't know you were coming over. It's great to see you."

"Gavin, I'm so glad you're here. This is my friend, Cece. I brought her over to show her where my father worked and to introduce her to Tommy. Cece, this is Gavin Connelly, the CEO of ArcTron."

"Nice to meet you, Cece," he said. "Any friend of Kathryn's is a friend of mine."

Tommy appeared in the hallway, tucking his wrinkled shirt into his pants. "Hey, Kathryn, glad you could make it," he said as he walked over and was introduced to Cece.

Gavin adjusted the large notebook he was carrying to the other arm. "I have an appointment, so I need to be going. Kathryn, it's always a pleasure to see you."

"You too."

After he left, Kate looked at Tommy. "Gavin seems awfully tired. Is he all right?"

Tommy shrugged. "He's been burning the midnight oil a lot lately. He negotiated a patent deal recently for some new product he came up with. It must have been a ton of hard work, but it paid off for him. Did you see his new Mercedes in the parking lot?"

Tommy took the women on a tour. They peeked into a couple of the offices and one of the electronics labs. Tommy's focus was the computer room, and he was obviously proud of the work he had done providing a state-of-the-art computer environment for the scientists who worked there.

"Do you know much about computers, Cece?" he asked.

"Absolutely nothing," she laughed. "You lost me when we crossed the threshold."

The two women followed Tommy into his office. His work area was as disheveled as he was. Computer magazines and books were piled everywhere, and he had to clean off a couple of chairs so the two women would have a place to sit. Diet soda cans lined his desk along with an empty wrapper from Arby's. "Sorry about the mess," he said as he swept the lunchtime remains into a wastebasket and settled into the chair behind his desk. "So, what made you two decide you want to help Representative Hodges with his campaign?"

"Not both of us. Just her," Cece said and gestured with her thumb toward Kathryn.

Kate squirmed in her seat. *Should I tell him? No, I can't afford for anybody else to know.* "Cece's not interested in politics. I just wanted to bring her by so she could see where Dad worked and to meet you."

"Great. I'm glad you both came. So, you're the one who's taken an interest in the Hodges campaign?"

"Yes, I'm really excited that I might meet him. I've never met a candidate for governor before." *I can't believe I'm looking straight into Tommy's eyes and misleading him. He's been my friend since kindergarten. I feel like such a creep.*

Tommy didn't seem to notice. "The headquarters building is just a few blocks from here. After you told me you were interested, I called and they confirmed that Hodges will be in the office this afternoon. We can walk over there now, and you'll probably get a chance to meet him in person."

"That would be great."

Tommy stood. "Well then, let's go. Cece, you're welcome to come if you like."

"No, thanks. Maybe some other time."

The three left through the back door of the building. Tommy and Kate walked Cece to her car and started toward Hodges's campaign headquarters.

So now I'm going to meet Robert Hodges, thought Kate. *I wonder if I can keep from choking him.*

CHAPTER 19

"**S**low down, Kathryn. I can't walk that fast."

Kate looked over her shoulder at her friend. Tommy was gasping for air as he tried to keep up. He reminded her of the chubby little boy she had gone to school with, and she had an urge to put her arm around him like she'd done in the third grade when some older boys had taunted him on the playground.

"Sorry," she said. "I didn't realize I was walking so fast."

"Remember, I'm not an athlete. I'm just a computer nerd." He put his index fingers on the sides of his head and pointed them around like antennae.

"Very funny. I guess I'm a little nervous about meeting Representative Hodges. I feel kind of silly since I don't really know anything about politics."

Tommy stopped to catch his breath. "So, what made you decide to get involved in a political campaign?"

Kate turned her face away from him, pretending to look at a mountain laurel bush next to the sidewalk. *Another lie.* "Um, it was just a spur-of-the-moment kind of thing. I saw one of his ads on TV and decided it was time to get involved in the process."

"Good for you. It's the best civics lesson you'll ever have," he said as they began to walk again, more slowly this time.

Tommy is so innocent. He must be the easiest person in the world to fool. She pushed back against the guilt that had bubbled up inside her. "Tell me something about Hodges. What's he like?" she asked.

Tommy stopped again, reached into his pocket and pulled out a coin. "He's a lot like this penny. The image is on one side. On the surface, Hodges is the easy-going, gracious guy you see in the campaign ads." He flipped the coin over. "But the other side is different. Underneath, he's very disciplined and driven. He pushes his campaign staff hard—sort of a take-no-prisoners type."

"What does that mean? 'Take-no-prisoners'?"

"He encourages and rewards good work, but he doesn't tolerate incompetence or laziness. I once heard him ream out a staff member for messing up a schedule. It wasn't pretty, and that guy finally quit."

Kate frowned. "That doesn't sound like the kind of person you'd be working for." *If you only knew the kind of person he really is, you'd quit too.*

"It's not his personality I support; it's his positions on the issues. He's a moderate thinker and represents the values of this state well. He's a huge supporter of the high-tech industry, and that's a direct benefit to us here in Bellevue. He can be a pretty tough cookie, but I believe he'd be a good governor."

They stopped on the corner to wait for the traffic light to change.

Kate tucked a strand of hair behind her ear. "I'm not eager to work in an environment where I could get yelled at for making a mistake."

"You don't have to worry about that as a volunteer. It's just the paid staff he holds accountable. The volunteers are treated with kid gloves." He tossed the penny in the air, caught it, and slapped it down on the back of his wrist. It came up heads. Tommy smiled and looked at Kate. "See, you'll only be dealing with the good side of Hodges."

As far as I'm concerned, there is no good side of Hodges.

They reached the campaign headquarters which was housed in an empty store in a small shopping center. There was a large banner hanging over the front door declaring, "Hodges for Governor."

Hodges for jerk of the century, thought Kate. She clenched her teeth and zeroed in on the goal. *Robert Hodges is a despicable human being, and this is my chance to find out as much as I can about him.*

CHAPTER 20

K ate followed Tommy into the building where a dozen or so men and women sat hunched over desks arranged around the walls of a large room. Five others stood in front of a whiteboard at the far end of the headquarters. One of them was pointing to an entry on the board and seemed to be explaining something to the others. Kate could make out the names of some counties listed on the board with numbers beside them.

Tommy greeted several of the folks he knew and asked a young lady behind the front desk if they could see Representative Hodges. After a minute, a tall, silver-haired man dressed in a light-blue golf shirt and tan slacks stepped out of a side office and into the main work area. His reading glasses hung on a cord around his neck. Kate recognized Robert Hodges and thought he looked older and somewhat thinner in person than on the TV ads she had seen.

A woman carrying a laptop followed him out of his office. She was dressed fashionably in a burgundy pantsuit and her hair was pulled back in a severe bun. She stopped at the receptionist's desk while Hodges strode toward the newcomers, covering the room with just a few steps. "Tommy, good to see you again."

Tommy is on a first name basis with Representative Hodges? Who would have thought that? Kate looked closely at Hodges. Although he was smiling, Kate sensed a tension about him, like a compressed spring. And something in his voice sounded insincere. She couldn't imagine her lovely mother with this man. *Could the Goldmans be wrong?*

Tommy motioned toward Kate. "Representative Hodges, I'd like you to meet my friend, Kathryn Frasier. She might be interested in volunteering for your campaign."

Hodges faced Kate, and she thought his expression changed slightly, from welcoming to curious. "Kathryn Frasier?"

Does he recognize the name?

He seemed to be trying to remember something. "By any chance are you related to Mary Ann Frasier of Randall County? She's one of our largest donors."

"No, I don't know her." *Is he probing? Trying to get more information?*

"Well, I'm glad you stopped by," Hodges said, and his expression became amiable again. "We can always use good volunteers on the campaign. Tell me, do your parents live in the area?"

Why would he ask that? In the warm room, Kate felt a drop of perspiration slide down the side of her face.

Before she had a chance to answer, Tommy leaned in and said in a low voice, "Unfortunately, Kathryn's parents died in an automobile accident in Nevada a few months ago. Maybe you knew them: Bill and Leah Frasier?"

Kate gulped. She hadn't counted on Tommy's giving information about her parents.

"Bill and Leah Frasier?" Hodges looked at Kate with an expression of concern. "No. No, I don't think I knew them. I'm so sorry for your loss. Please accept my condolences."

Does he know? Or is he just sincerely expressing sympathy?

"Thank you," she managed.

The woman with the laptop joined the group. "Liz, we have a new prospective volunteer," Hodges said. "Kathryn Frasier, this is Elizabeth Howley, my personal assistant."

She nodded in Kathryn's direction. "Nice to meet you," she said, but she didn't look pleased at all. Kate smiled and nodded back.

A man with straight black hair sticking up in all directions burst out of a side room and darted around the lobby, pausing a couple of times to speak to staffers. "Don, don't forget to get the latest poll numbers to me by four o'clock. And Jennie, I need the updated list of Bellevue volunteers at the same time." Spotting the little group, he practically jogged over to them.

Hodges introduced him. "Jeremy, meet Kathryn Frasier. She may be interested in volunteering with our campaign. Kathryn, this is Jeremy Dodd, my campaign manager and the best one around."

After a brief minute of small talk, Jeremy reminded Hodges of a phone interview scheduled to begin in ten minutes.

"I'll take it in your office," Hodges said, and then addressed Kate again with what sounded like a well-rehearsed motivational speech. "Kathryn, I'm delighted you came by. I encourage you to research the issues in this campaign and decide if you want to support us. If you do, we would appreciate your help on the campaign."

As Kate watched Hodges, Elizabeth, and Jeremy disappear into a side office, she heard a voice behind her. "Hey, Tommy."

* * *

Kate turned to see a man entering through the outer door.

"Good to see you, my friend," he said as he clapped Tommy on the shoulder, then extended his hand to Kate. "Hi. I'm Mike Strickland, Representative Hodges's chief of staff."

He looked very professional in a gray pin-striped suit, but his voice was warm and pleasant. He had dark hair, dark eyes, and a heart-melting smile. Kate noticed several young women in the room paying close attention to his arrival.

Wow. The chief of staff. I'm meeting all the bigwigs here. Kate took his hand. "I'm Kathryn Frasier. I'm thinking about volunteering for the campaign."

"Well, that's great. We need all the help we can get, right Tommy?" He raised his eyebrows at Tommy and grinned before he addressed Kate again. "Have you filled out one of the volunteer forms? It's just a formality, really. The usual stuff: name, address, bank account balance." They all laughed lightly.

Very smooth, thought Kate.

"I'll get one of the forms for you," Tommy said. He walked across the room to a table stacked with papers and clipboards.

Mike leaned against the door jamb and crossed his arms over his chest. "So, tell me about yourself, Kathryn. Are you new to Bellevue?"

"No, I grew up here and just moved back a few years ago for my job."

"Oh? Where do you work?"

"I'm a software developer at Vectra Corporation. Right now, I'm on a leave of absence, but I plan to return to work in a few weeks."

"Software developer? Now you're talking. We could use some extra technical expertise."

"Actually, I haven't made up my mind for sure about volunteering. I'll think about it and let you know." *But you'd never guess the real reason I'm here.*

"Great. We'd like to have you on the team. Take that form with you and, if you decide you'd like to work with us, fill it out and return it to this office. I promise you that working on a political campaign will not be dull."

Tommy came back with the application and handed it to Kate.

"By the way," Mike said, "we're having a big rally on Saturday in Center Square. You should stop by."

"Thanks. Maybe I will."

"Good. Hope to see you there," he said and walked into Jeremy's office.

Tommy headed for the door. "If you're ready, I have to get back to the office."

"Sure. Let's go." Kate followed him out. *So, I have met the enemy. Now what?*

CHAPTER 21

K ate put the volunteer application in her purse. "Campaign headquarters was different than I thought it would be."

"Oh? How so?" Tommy asked.

"I didn't expect to meet the senior staff members. And I was surprised that everybody knows you so well. Have you known Representative Hodges long?"

Tommy chuckled. "He didn't even know I existed until a few months ago. They were having problems setting up their website for the campaign, and I ironed things out for them. He heard about it, and he's been real friendly to me ever since. He offered to hire me full-time for the duration of the campaign, but I can't work at ArcTron and work for him at the same time. Still, they're all real nice to me." He made the little antenna gesture with his hands again. "Being a computer geek comes in handy sometimes."

As they continued down the sidewalk, Kate asked, "What's your opinion of Hodges? As a person, I mean. Does he have a family?" *And has he told them about his past?*

Tommy shrugged. "I've never heard him talk about a family. All I know is that he's divorced. The only people who are really close to him are the key three."

"The key three?"

"The folks that you met today are what the rest of the staff call 'the key three.'"

"Why do they call them that?"

"Because they're one hundred percent devoted to Hodges and they all have complete access to him. Elizabeth Howley has been with him forever. She worked for him on his first campaign for public office, and she's very protective of him, like a gatekeeper.

They say he doesn't make any decisions about hiring or firing without consulting her first."

"That's interesting. I definitely had the feeling that she didn't like me being there, like I was some kind of interloper. I felt a little uneasy."

"Don't worry. She's does that with everybody. It's like she's suspicious of people's motives or something." Tommy touched Kate's elbow. "Hey, slow down. You're beginning that race-walk thing again."

"Sorry." Kate slowed her pace. "Tell me about the others I met today—Mike and Jeremy."

"Well, they're a real interesting pair. They have to work together, but they don't seem to like each other very much."

"Why is that?"

"I don't know. Maybe because they're such different personalities. Mike's a cool guy, and you can tell Hodges really likes him, even though he's a lot younger. He's got a talent for talking to people and getting them to open up and feel comfortable. That makes him very valuable when they're convincing the big money guys to fund the campaign. They say Mike can be in a room with a hundred people, but if he's talking to you, you'll feel like you're the only one there."

"And Jeremy?"

"Well, Jeremy is a real piece of work. This is the first time he's been in charge of a campaign, and I think he's operating on overdrive to make sure they win. He's almost manic the way he runs around getting everything worked out. Of the three of them, I think he's the most committed to this run for governor. I once heard him say—kidding, of course—that he would kill to get Hodges elected governor."

Is that so?

G avin Connelly was just pulling into the parking lot when Kate and Tommy got back to ArcTron.

"That's his new car?" Kate asked. "It's beautiful."

Tommy nodded. "Yeah. Mercedes Benz S-Class. I bet that set him back a penny or two."

As Gavin climbed out of the car, they walked over to him.

"How'd your meeting go?" Gavin asked.

"It was . . . very interesting," she said. "I met Hodges and some of his senior staff members."

"That's great. I hear they're having a big rally for Hodges on Saturday. Are you going?"

Kate nodded. "Yes, I think I'll go. I've never been to a political rally before, and now that I've met the candidate, it'll be meaningful to be there. Are you planning to go, Gavin?"

"No. I'm on my way out of town tomorrow morning. I've decided to take the new car on the road. I've never been to Reno before, and it's about a five-hour drive. Should be a good chance to break in the car."

"Are you a gambler?"

"No. I've only gambled a couple of times in my life. Seems silly to work hard for your money and then throw it away in a casino. I'll just take in a couple of shows and eat the good food there. I'll be back Sunday evening, but it'll be nice to get away for a couple of days." He locked his car. "I just stopped back in to pick up my laptop. You have the master key to the offices, Tommy. Just call me if there are any issues."

"No problem. Have a good trip. I'll see you next week."

Gavin left the two friends and went into the office building.

Kate had noticed Tommy pulling at his ear and shuffling his feet during the conversation, a sure sign he was worried about something. And Gavin hadn't looked directly at Tommy, even when he was talking to him. Something wasn't right between the two of them. "You okay?" she asked Tommy. "You look a little nervous."

"To be honest with you, Kathryn, I think Gavin wants to fire me."

"Fire you?" Kate frowned at this surprise announcement. "Why would he want to do that?"

"We had a glitch in the computer system a few months ago. We lost a bunch of emails, and I haven't been able to figure out what happened. Gavin is real strict about doing things by the book, and he wasn't happy about losing all those emails. Besides, he knows a lot about system administration. He actually worked on the computers here at ArcTron before his dad made him the CEO. I know there has to be a logical explanation, but I haven't found it yet. I'd hate to get fired from my first real job."

"I'm sure you're worried about nothing. No sane person would fire the best system administrator on the planet," she said.

* * *

After Kate left, Tommy went to his office, closed the door, and opened his laptop. Tapping away, he softly sang a mischievous lyric to a familiar melody.

A bit, a byte
I'm working day and night
I'll get you yet,
My little pet.
I'll put a bit into your byte.

CHAPTER 23

"You did a great job in that radio interview." Mike followed Hodges back to his office.

"Yeah, I was happy with it," Hodges said absent-mindedly and walked behind his desk. He picked up a few notes the receptionist had left and shuffled through them.

Strange, thought Mike. *Bob doesn't usually seem preoccupied, but today he looks like his mind is in another world. Wonder what's going on.*

Hodges put the notes down on his desk and looked at Mike. "How did things go with the business folks today? Did we get some solid pledges?"

Mike leaned back against one of the tables with his ankles crossed. "We got a couple of commitments, but most of the big donors are reluctant to jump on board until they see the poll numbers moving in our direction. I'll keep working on them, but it's all going to depend on the campaign gaining some momentum."

"I agree. I'm counting on this rally to give us a boost. The folks here are excited about it."

"Let's hope that lights the fire." Mike took his phone out of his pocket and checked his calendar. "By the way, you're scheduled to speak to the Rotary Club at seven o'clock tonight. Since Jeremy's taking tonight off, I'll be with you at the dinner. If there's nothing else, I'll head back to the hotel and get some email out of the way. I'll meet you at the hotel at six-thirty."

"Before you go, there is something else I want to talk to you about." Hodges sat down in his desk chair and folded his hands together. "What do you know about that young woman who was just here—Kathryn Frasier?"

Kathryn Frasier?

* * *

Barkley greeted Kate with excited yaps when she got home. He bounced around the living room, his way of saying he was ready to go to the park. "Okay, boy, we'll go in a minute."

She was changing into her running clothes when Cece called. "How'd your visit to Hodges's office go? Remember, you agreed to tell me everything."

Kate put her phone on speaker so she could talk and dress at the same time. "I had a chance to meet Hodges and talk to him for a few minutes. They're having a big rally for him on Saturday and Tommy's setting up the AV equipment, so I'll probably go just to see what it's like."

"What did you think of him?"

Kate sat on the edge of the bed and pulled on a pair of socks. "I don't know what to think, Cece. He was pleasant enough, but it all seemed sort of . . . artificial."

"Do you think he knows anything about your parents or about the accident?"

Kate slipped her feet into running shoes. "I got the feeling that he made some kind of connection when Tommy mentioned my parents' names, but maybe I was just imagining it. I did learn something that might be useful, though. Is your mom there? I'd like to ask her a question."

"Sure. Mom's right here. I'll put us on speaker."

Sylvia's voice came across. "Kathryn, how are you? Cece told me that you went to meet Robert Hodges. I hope that wasn't too much of a strain for you."

"Hi, Mrs. Goldman. Yes, I went to the campaign headquarters today and met him. I also met one of his staff members, a woman who has worked for him since his first campaign, and I remembered that you said my mother worked on his first campaign too."

"That's right."

"Do you remember Mother mentioning someone named Elizabeth Howley?"

There was a brief silence before Sylvia responded, "No, I'm sorry. It was a long time ago. I don't remember that name."

"Maybe that's her married name. Hang on. I'll look her up." Kate got her laptop from the dresser and did an Internet search for Elizabeth Howley. "There's an entry for her in Wikipedia. It looks like her maiden name was Hart. Does that ring a bell? Elizabeth Hart?"

"Yes, I do remember that name. Your mother mentioned someone named Liz Hart. It made an impression on me because your mother said she should have been named Liz Heartless because she was so mean. From what your mother said, I sensed that this Liz person may have had a lot of influence over Robert Hodges. Of course, that's just an impression. Did you say you met her? What did you think?"

"She didn't say much, but she made me feel uneasy. I think she also overheard Tommy mention my parents' names. I wonder if it meant anything to her."

"I don't know, but I'm very proud of you that you had the strength of character to meet Robert Hodges and talk to him. I'm sure it wasn't easy for you to be in his presence."

"Thanks, Mrs. Goldman. You've been very helpful."

Cece broke in. "Are you okay?"

"Yes, I'm fine. My brain just feels a little cluttered, like a house that needs a good cleaning. I'm going to take Barkley out to the park and spend some time running to clear my head."

After she hung up, Kate read through the rest of the Wikipedia entry. Elizabeth Hart had married George Howley in 1990. He had died in 2002 in a rock climbing accident in Nevada. *Liz Heartless. Certainly seems to fill the bill.*

Kate loaded Barkley into the car and spent a thoughtful hour on the trails at Campbell Park, reviewing her trip to the campaign headquarters and meeting the staff members. Mike was pleasant enough, but Jeremy and Liz seemed disingenuous, like they were acting out parts in a play.

Robert Hodges was a special case. Every time she thought of him, a wave of anger washed over her, and she picked up her pace. Even the inimitable Barkley seemed relieved when they headed back to the car.

When they got home, she found her phone on the kitchen island. There was a message from Phil Warren. "Doggone it," she said. "How did I manage to forget my phone when I went out to run?"

His message said her car was ready and could be picked up the following morning. There was a worn belt that should be replaced, but they didn't have one in stock, so they'd arrange another appointment when she could bring it back in for a short repair. "Stop by my office and say hello when you come in," he said. His voice sounded friendly and inviting.

Kate listened to the message a second time as she took a lasagna dinner out of the freezer. She recalled the way he had teased her about the note. And the way he looked at her as if seeing her as a woman for the first time. Her face grew warm at the thought of him. *But he couldn't possibly be interested in me. Could he?*

CHAPTER 24

Friday

"Is Phil in?" Kate asked as she handed the keys of the loaner car over to Maclean on Friday morning.

"I think he's in his office with someone."

She glanced over and saw that his office door was closed. Kate walked to the cashier's desk and got in line behind two women. She fidgeted, transferring her weight from one foot to the other as she waited to pay. And she kept looking back at Phil's door.

The women in front of her were apparently good friends and were gushing over each other's clothes. Finally, they finished their business and, as they moved away, Kate heard one of them say, "The first day I get a chance, I'm going to treat myself to a new wardrobe."

Kate stared off into space. *The first day. Behold the first day. But the first day of what?*

The cashier cleared her throat noisily. "Can I help you?"

"Oh yes. Sorry," said Kate. She paid her bill and picked up the keys to her car. When she looked back, she saw Phil walk out of his office with an attractive young woman at his side. They were laughing and talking. Kate started down the corridor toward them when she saw Phil pull the woman close and give her a long, affectionate hug. Kate quickly did a U-turn, exited through the outside door, and jogged across the parking lot.

Stop acting like a silly schoolgirl, she chided herself. *This handsome guy flirts with you just once, and you want to make it into a romance. Grow up. He probably flirts with every woman he meets. Phil Warren is definitely not the kind of person you should be interested in.* But before she got in her car, she looked back, hoping to catch sight of him. He wasn't there.

CHAPTER 25

Kate arrived at the Goldmans' apartment Friday evening with a bottle of red wine and a bouquet of flowers. Cece answered the door and escorted her into the large living/dining area. An appetizing aroma of roast beef permeated the room.

"We're so glad you could come, Kathryn," Sylvia said as she came out of the kitchen and put a bowl of mashed potatoes on the table. "The Shabbat dinner is our favorite meal of the week. Some of our rituals may be unusual to you, but we'll explain why we do everything as we go along."

"Thank you, Mrs. Goldman. I've never been to a Shabbat dinner before, and I'm looking forward to it."

Harry checked his watch. "It's just about sunset, so let's begin."

Sylvia and Harry sat at opposite ends of the dining room table while Kate and Cece faced each other from the sides. A decorative cloth covered a basket of bread in the center of the table and two candlesticks stood next to the bread.

Sylvia lit the candles, covered her eyes and prayed, first in Hebrew, then in English. "Blessed art Thou, O Lord our God, King of the universe, who has set us apart by Your commandments and has enjoined upon us the kindling of the Sabbath light." She gently waved her hands over the candles, and Kate could feel their warmth.

Harry prayed over the wine and then poured it into the glasses. Each one took a sip. It tasted sweet and good. He uncovered the bread and continued his prayer. As they passed the loaf around, each person broke off a piece. It was fresh and warm and crusty.

While they helped themselves to the rest of the food, Harry explained, "As Jews, we believe Sabbath begins at sunset on

Friday evening and concludes at sunset Saturday evening. The Sabbath is God's holy day, and we honor it by ceasing from work and resting as He commanded. We light the candles to welcome the Sabbath into our home. The bread is a special kind called challah. These traditions have been practiced for thousands of years."

For months, Kate's diet had consisted of simple salads, take-outs, and microwaveables. This delicious home-cooked meal was a real treat. "Mrs. Goldman, this is wonderful!"

The meal proceeded with cheerful conversation. Cece described her job working in her father's jewelry store. "My favorite part of the job is repairing watches," she grinned, holding up her left wrist with the watch from the fencepost while everyone at the table laughed. "But I'm an actress at heart, and my real love is performing in local stage productions on the side."

Sylvia and Harry told the story of how they met, and Sylvia brought out some old pictures of them as newlyweds.

Over a special cherries jubilee dessert, Kate said, "You know, a week ago I was an orphan without a single relative in the world. Now I find I have a sister. And, since you're her parents, I guess that makes you my aunt and uncle."

"That's exactly the way we feel," Sylvia said as she reached over and patted Kate's hand.

Harry's smile faded. "We know something in our family about orphans. You see, Sylvia and I both lost our parents in the Holocaust."

Kate looked back and forth between Harry and Sylvia. These two people had shown her so much kindness and hospitality, she never would have guessed they had suffered such horror. "I'm so sorry."

Sylvia placed her napkin on the table and folded her hands in her lap. "It's terribly sad, isn't it, that each of us at this table has lost parents through tragedy, although in different ways.

"Harry and I were both born in Eastern Europe toward the end of World War II. As the fighting wound down, the Nazis were furiously rounding up Jews, trying to finish off their horrendous genocide before they lost the war. My parents asked a young Christian couple they knew to keep me—I was less than a year old—until they returned. They never came back. That Christian couple risked their lives for me and eventually brought me to the United States, declaring I was their child.

"They heard that some rabbis were looking for Jewish children who were lost in the war, and they contacted them to see if my original parents could be located. My actual parents had been murdered, but this wonderful couple gave me up for adoption to a Jewish family in New York because they felt they could not stand in the way of my upbringing. My new family raised me as their own. It's odd how much I have in common with Cece, isn't it?"

"My story is similar," Harry said as he put his coffee cup down. "My parents also asked a couple to take me, and they brought me to America. There were good people in Europe who took terrible risks to help the helpless, and we were able to build new lives here. Sylvia and I believe God led us to each other and eventually He gave us Cece as our most wonderful gift."

Kate's eyes welled with tears. "I had the good fortune to know my parents for twenty-seven years, while you never knew yours at all. Aren't you bitter over what happened? Aren't you angry that you never had the chance to know them?"

Sylvia and Harry exchanged a long look. Sylvia sighed and answered. "We're not angry or bitter. Of course we're terribly sad that our parents never had the chance to live their lives, and we're hurt that we don't even know what happened to them. We've both dealt with a sense of guilt that we had good upbringings by very good adoptive parents while our own parents must surely have died terrible deaths."

Harry put his elbows on the table and rested his chin on his hands. "Kathryn, have you ever heard of the concept of *Tikkun Olam*?"

"No, I don't think so."

"Tikkun Olam literally means 'repairing the world.' It holds that by helping others, we will improve society and show honor to God. There is evil in the world, to be sure, and sometimes it has to be fought with armies and weapons. But it also has to be fought every day with acts of kindness toward our friends and even our enemies. Sylvia and I believe we honor the memory of our parents by trying to live our lives according to these principles."

Kate considered what he had said. "So, you're saying we should try to repair the world through acts of goodness?"

"That's basically it. We believe God has a plan for the world and, even though we don't know what that is, we think He has a role for us to play, and it's up to us to do our part."

Sylvia smiled tenderly. "Now you understand why we're here in Bellevue. To be left alone is a terrible thing, and we want so much for you and Cece to have each other as family. Also, we know what it's like to lose family members to the forces of evil. If there's any chance that someone deliberately caused harm to your parents, we want to help you find out. It's not out of revenge—nothing like that. But we feel it's important to know the truth so that justice can be served, if possible."

Harry said, "It's our way of bringing light into the world to overcome the darkness. Light symbolizes goodness. You remember God created light on the first day of creation."

Cece suddenly slapped the side of her face with her open hand and looked at Kate with bulging eyes. "That's it! The first day. God created light on the first day. The note must have something to do with light."

Kate gasped. "Yes! 'Behold the first day.' The word *behold* must be a clue that it's a biblical reference, and *the first day* must mean it has to do with light."

"What are you two talking about?" asked Sylvia. "What's all this about 'Behold the first day'?"

Cece explained the clue Kathryn had found on her car.

"Oh my goodness," said Sylvia as she put her coffee cup back down and dabbed at her mouth with her napkin. "Do you think this could be related to your parents' accident?"

"I don't know, but I think we just made a big step forward," said Kate. "Thanks to you, Mr. Goldman, we know more about the clue."

"Would it help to know the exact verse?" Harry asked. He got a Bible down from the mantle and read from the book of Genesis. "And God said, 'Let there be light,' and there was light. And God saw that the light was good. And God separated the light from the darkness. God called the light Day, and the darkness He called Night. And there was evening and there was morning, the first day."

"So, it must have to do with light," Kate murmured.

"But what kind of light?" Harry asked. "Candles? Light bulbs? The sun? There's a lot to choose from."

Kate gazed at the chandelier above the table. "I don't know, but something will turn up."

Sylvia chuckled as she stood and began clearing the table. "I hope you solve it soon. None of us will be able to sleep until we know the answer to your puzzle."

* * *

A little after midnight, Kate awoke to the sound of distant thunder. The numbers on the digital clock next to her bed were blinking. Barkley was standing next to his doggie bed, whimpering softly.

"It's okay, boy. The electricity must have gone off, but it's back on now." She flipped on the bedside lamp, patted the little dog on his head, and reset the clock. "Go back to your bed. I'll get the flashlight just in case we lose electricity again." She got a large flashlight down from the bookcase next to her bed and set it on her night table.

"Everything's fine. Go back to sleep now," she said as she turned off the lamp and lay down. Ten seconds later, she sat up in bed with a big smile on her face.

"Very clever, Dad."

CHAPTER 26

Saturday

Kate was still smiling when she called Cece at seven o'clock, the earliest she figured she could get away with on a Saturday morning.

"Hullo?" came the sleepy voice on the other end of the line.

"I figured it out."

"Figured what out?" The slurred words were accompanied by a yawn.

"I know what the clue means."

"Really?" Cece's voice was suddenly alert. "How did you figure it out? What does it mean?"

"When my power went out last night, I got my flashlight, and I found the next clue."

"I don't get it."

"When I was a little girl and the electricity went off at night, my father would bring out his big flashlight. He'd gather the three of us together in a room, and guess what he'd say?"

"I have no idea."

"He'd say, 'Let there be light.' Then he'd switch the flashlight on and say, 'And then there was light.' "

Cece squealed in delight. "That's amazing. It has to do with the flashlight! So, what's the new clue?"

"Can you come over this morning? I'll show you."

"If you make the coffee, I'll be there in thirty minutes."

When Cece arrived, the two women hugged each other glee-fully. Cece took a small slip of paper out of her purse and handed it to Kathryn. "When I told my father about it, he jotted down this note to you. It's a quote from the Bible."

The slip of paper read, "Light dawns in the darkness for the upright. —Psalm 112"

Kate shook her head in awe. "Wow. That's incredibly ap-propriate," she said. "Does your father have the entire Bible memorized?"

"I don't know. Probably." Cece shrugged. "Now show me what you found." Her blue eyes twinkled.

Kate handed her the flashlight. "Shine it on the wall."

Cece pointed the flashlight and flicked the switch. "It didn't come on. Is the battery dead?"

"Nope. The battery is fine. The flashlight did come on."

Cece tilted her head to one side, thought for a second, and then turned the flashlight toward her. "No wonder it didn't shine on the wall. It's covered with a piece of paper."

The writing on the paper said, "Check the flower box."

"Oh my goodness," Cece squealed again and jumped up and down. "Your father is so clever."

"Yeah. This is exactly the kind of thing he loved to do."

"Where's the flower box? Does your house have a flower box?"

"No. But that would be too obvious. He had something else in mind. Let's eat breakfast and try to come up with something."

While Kate was setting the oatmeal and coffee on the table, Cece asked, "Do you think it could be a box in one of the flower beds around your home?"

"I doubt it, but it's worth a walk around the house." After breakfast, the girls trekked around the landscaping, poking at the bushes, but there was no box.

Cece's phone alarm started playing music. "Oops," she said. "I have to go. I have a couple of errands to run this morning. What are you doing today?"

"I'm going to the big political rally for Hodges this afternoon. I'm hoping I can get some more information about him while I'm there. And maybe I'll get some inspiration about the new clue."

CHAPTER 27

So, this is what a political rally looks like.

Red, white, and blue balloons were tied to a platform that had been erected in the middle of the square across the street from the Bellevue Center Office Building. Colorful banners waved gently from corner lampposts under a clear, azure sky. Although the breeze was cool and the ground was still damp from the overnight rain, bright sunshine warmed the mass of people streaming into the plaza.

With the band playing a lively tune, Kate felt caught up in the goodwill all around her as she threaded her way through the crowd to the platform where Tommy Abrahams was working on the microphones. She put her hands on the edge of the stage and looked up at him. "Hi Tommy. How's it going?"

"Hey Kathryn." He squatted down at the edge of the stage so they could hear each other over the noise of the audience. "Everything's working fine. I just have a couple of things to double-check. Whaddya think about all this?"

"Pretty amazing. There must be close to a thousand people here."

"Yeah. That's what I'd guess."

"Where's Representative Hodges and his staff?" she asked.

He pointed to the office building behind her. "Hodges, Liz, and Mike are over there meeting with the big-name supporters." He cocked his thumb in the opposite direction. "Jeremy is behind the stage, giving the volunteers their last-minute instructions. I have to stay close by in case we have any AV issues. Maybe I'll see you afterward."

"Okay. Good luck." Kate walked around to the back of the platform in time to hear Jeremy's pep talk to the volunteers.

"Listen up, guys." Jeremy motioned the little group of volunteers to gather around him. "We've got a perfect day and a fantastic bunch of supporters out here. I'm counting on you to make this an A-plus rally for our candidate. Just remember: it's all about the image, so make eye contact and keep smiling." He illustrated by lifting the corners of his mouth with his index fingers. "They need to know we care about them, so show 'em you love 'em. They'll remember that on election day."

He pointed to the space underneath the speaker's platform. "If you need more bumper stickers or hats to hand out, they're all stored here under the stage. Now be sure to spread out so you connect with every single person."

As the volunteers dispersed with their giveaways, Jeremy bounded over to the office building.

Kate roamed through the crowd, looking for people she knew. She recognized several of her coworkers from Vectra Software Corporation and a couple of professors from the university. She found herself looking for Phil Warren. *Why am I still thinking about him?* But she continued to scan the multitude around her for his face.

A volunteer was weaving through the audience, giving out "Vote for Hodges. Vote for Progress." bumper stickers. Kate took one and put it in her purse.

An Anglican nun dressed in a gray habit brushed against Kate as she passed by. "Excuse me," she mumbled.

"No problem," Kate responded. As she watched the woman hurry off, she noticed something that took her breath away. The nun was wearing a familiar gold watch on her left wrist.

Cece?

Before Kate could follow the nun, a man standing beside her exclaimed in a loud voice, "Look. There they are." He was pointing to the office building next to the square.

Kate watched as a small group of men and women paraded across the street toward the stage. Liz Howley and Jeremy Dodd led the way, followed by seven or eight others. *They must be the people who are going to declare their support for Hodges today.*

Kate stood on tiptoe and craned her neck to see if she recognized any of them. She saw former governor Sparks wearing his trademark flannel shirt and waving enthusiastically.

It took the little troop a few minutes to wind through the large assembly. As Kate watched them climb the stairs to the platform, she heard a low voice behind her.

"Hello there."

CHAPTER 28

"Glad to see you could make it to our little party." Mike Strickland was standing just behind her and smiling.

Kate smiled back, glad to have the company. "I'm surprised to see you out here, Mike. I thought you'd be with Representative Hodges. Doesn't he need you with him?"

"Not at all. Liz handles all the logistics, and Jeremy is the head cheerleader. I just wander around looking for pretty girls to talk into volunteering on our campaign." He winked.

Kate blushed. *Charming. No wonder he's in politics.*

"So, what do you think about all this?" he asked.

"It's pretty lively. I was surprised there are so many people here. Is the rally going to be very long?"

"It's just a chance for Hodges to introduce himself to the community and show how much support he has. His speech will be short—only about thirty minutes—and no real details. Just broad brushstrokes about why the nice folks of Bellevue should vote for him." He gestured at the masses of people surrounding them. "Political rallies are kind of fun, though, don't you think?"

"It reminds me of some of the races I've run. A bunch of people milling around, waiting for things to start."

"I guess this is just another kind of race, but there's a lot at stake in this one." Mike touched her elbow and pointed to the stage. "Looks like we're getting ready to start. Almost on time too. That's something of a miracle. Do you know any of those folks up on the stage?"

"I recognize Governor Sparks. And I know Dean Jefferson. He's the dean of the engineering school where my father used to work. I don't know any of the others."

"They're all movers and shakers in the state. Hodges was happy they came out to show their support. The rally should be a big story on the evening news tonight, and that'll give us a real boost. I wouldn't be surprised if our poll numbers jump two or three points."

Elizabeth approached the microphone and placed a yellow folder on the podium. "Good afternoon," she said as she adjusted the microphone down to her height and paused until all the dignitaries made their way onto the stage and found their seats. After the buzz from the people in the square died down, she continued. "I want to welcome all of you to this rally in support of the campaign of Representative Robert Hodges for governor." Applause from the spectators. Kate clapped politely.

"I'm Elizabeth Howley, Representative Hodges's personal assistant, and I am honored to be here in Bellevue. First, let me introduce former governor George H. Sparks, who will give us some brief comments."

The crowd broke into a chant of "Sparky, Sparky" as the popular former governor stepped up to the microphone. He held up his hands to quiet the audience.

"Thank you, Elizabeth, and thank you to the great citizens of Bellevue. I am delighted to be back in this beautiful city. I always said that the folks in Bellevue could do anything, and I really appreciate the way you arranged the perfect weather for this rally."

There was laughter and more applause.

While Sparks continued his speech, Kate looked around for the nun who had walked past her, but she had disappeared. When she turned back, Sparks was just coming to the point.

"I've been trying to talk Robert Hodges into running for governor for the past couple of election cycles, and I am delighted that he has finally taken my advice. Ladies and gentlemen, without further ado, please welcome a great American, a great United States Representative and our next governor, Robert Hodges."

The band played the state anthem while Hodges strode out of the office building, across the street, and into the square. People swarmed around him, pressing in, trying to shake his hand, and it took a full five minutes before he maneuvered his way through the crowd and onto the stage.

While the band played and the audience applauded, he shook hands with each of the supporters on the platform. He faced the large assemblage in the square and waved to the spectators. He had on a blue dress shirt, open at the throat, with sleeves rolled up to his elbows, giving the impression that he was relaxed, fit, and ready to get to work. *Looks like the nicest guy in the world, the kind you'd like to invite to a family picnic. If they only knew.*

The crowd ramped up to a raucous applause and began cheering "USA, USA." Many waved small American flags.

After letting them have their way for a minute, Hodges held up his hands for quiet. Eventually the people in the square quieted down and the supporters on the stage took their seats.

Hodges put a hand on each side of the podium and leaned in toward the microphone. Looking out over the mass of faces, he said in a loud voice, "Hello, Bellevue!"

The people on the stage stood up again and the spectators restarted their applause. Many of the attendees snapped pictures and recorded videos.

"This is why he's so appealing to voters." Mike leaned over to Kate and half-shouted in her ear so that he could be heard over the noise of the crowd, as they watched Hodges waving and pointing into the audience, clearly enjoying himself. "He comes across as a genuine person, a regular guy, somebody you'd like to know personally. And he just loves being on that stage."

Kate tried to maintain a pleasant expression on her face. *What a phony.*

As the noise began to die down, someone standing in front of the stage held up a baby for Hodges to kiss. Everyone's eyes were on him as he put his arms out in a gesture of embrace and leaned over toward the child.

There was a loud popping sound, like a balloon breaking. Then someone screamed.

CHAPTER 29

Hodges spun around and fell backward into the men seated behind him. Everyone on the stage hit the floor, and the people in the square starting running in all directions. Kate was shoved hard from behind and fell face-first into the grass. Her right arm was pinned under her, but her left one was free, and she used it to push back against the man who was on top of her.

"Kathryn, be still." It was Mike Strickland who was holding her down.

"Get off," she sputtered, spitting out dirt and grass. "You're hurting me."

"Just be still until we know what's going on."

From her position, she could see some people running, their eyes wide with panic. Others were lying flat. "What's happening, Mike? Was that a gunshot?"

"I'm not sure."

After a few seconds, he stood and helped her up. He took her hand, and the two of them ran across the street to the shade of the office building where a large group of people had taken refuge.

"Are you all right?" Mike held her by her shoulders.

"My arm hurts where I fell on it. And I bumped my head on the ground." She felt warm blood oozing from her lip, and she wiped her mouth with the back of her hand.

"Here, take this." He handed her a monogrammed handkerchief.

She took it and wiped the side of her face. It came back covered with dirt, grass, and a little blood. "I'm okay. What happened?"

"It sounded like a gunshot." He looked across the street at the gaily decorated platform, now covered with police. A group of people leaned over someone who lay prone on the stage behind the podium. "I think they got Hodges."

Oh no. Even a brute like Hodges doesn't deserve to be gunned down.

"Stay here, okay? I need to get to him," Mike said.

"Yes, of course. Be careful."

As Mike ran across the plaza to his candidate, Kate wiped the side of her face again and wondered what she should do. She didn't like the idea of leaving the area. If the shooter was still around, she would be defenseless out in the open. Besides, she never did like the idea of running away, so she moved as close as she could to the side of the building.

Police sirens combined with a chorus of confused voices to fill the air around her. Some people were sobbing. Some looked dazed. Others were talking frantically. "Who got shot?" "Did they kill him?"

Most of the people had left the large platform where Hodges had been speaking, but Kate could make out Jeremy pointing to the office building while he talked to a policeman, as if trying to pinpoint where the shot came from. Mike had his arm around Elizabeth who was leaning over the still figure of Robert Hodges.

Medics put Hodges onto a gurney and rolled him into a waiting ambulance. It was impossible to see what condition he was in from where Kate stood. She saw Mike get into the ambulance with him.

A group of policemen came down the sidewalk and motioned everyone into the building. They questioned each person about what they saw, where they were standing, and whether they had been taking photos or videos during the rally. When an officer got to Kate, he wanted to know why her face was dirty and bleeding.

She explained how Mike had pushed her down to protect her. "Do you know who did this?" she asked.

"No, ma'am. But don't worry. We'll find him—or her."

When Kate was allowed to leave the area, she drove home and switched on the local news. The police had created a communications site at the hospital, and Police Commissioner Gerald Blake was making an announcement.

Blake's voice was authoritative and calm. "At this time, we believe one bullet was fired, probably from the office building across the street from the rally. Representative Hodges was hit in the right shoulder, but his wound is not serious. He is expected to recover fully and be released from the hospital in a day or two. We do not know the identity of the shooter or his motive for firing at Representative Hodges. If anyone has information about this assault, please contact the police department's special line set up for this case. The phone number is shown on the screen. I repeat, we need the public's help to track down the person who committed this heinous and cowardly act, so contact us immediately if you have any information."

As Blake stepped away from the microphone, the communications director asked Mike Strickland to give the public the latest status on Representative Hodges's condition. Mike appeared cool and controlled as he stepped to the microphone and put his hands on the podium. He had loosened his tie and Kate could see the dirt and grass stains on his white dress shirt.

"Representative Hodges has asked me to thank the wonderful police here in Bellevue for their quick response, and all of the folks at Bellevue Hospital for their attention and help. He is awake and eager to get out of the hospital so he can continue his campaign. Thank you all for your support and your prayers."

* * *

Gunshots. In Bellevue. It seemed impossible.

Kate turned the TV off and sat on her couch with her head in her hands. Sensing her distress, Barkley put his little head on her knee and whimpered.

Her brain was spinning. Everything about the day had been so perfect. The band playing. Hundreds of people dancing and singing. Mike Strickland standing next to her, pointing out the people on the stage.

But then she remembered the nun with the gold watch and had a terrifying thought. *Was it Cece? Could Cece have fired that shot? No, that's not possible. You're so traumatized you're imagining things.*

But Hodges had wanted to end Cece's life before she was even born. Could Cece be paying him back? Getting revenge?

The phone rang and she jumped.

CHAPTER 30

"**K**athryn," Cece shrieked, "are you all right? I just heard about the shooting."

"I'm fine. I was at the rally, but I only know what I saw on the news. Hodges was shot, but they don't know who did it. They think it came from the building across the street."

"Do you know how bad it is? Is he going to recover?"

It's her father. "They say it's not serious and he should recover completely."

Should I ask her? I have to know. Kate stood and began to pace behind the couch. "Cece, was that you at the rally disguised as a nun?"

"Yeah. I decided that I really wanted to see him in person, but I knew I'd have to wear some kind of disguise because I'm still afraid he might recognize me as Leah's daughter. I borrowed that nun's habit from the local theater company. When I spotted you in the plaza, I bumped into you so you would know it was me, but I wasn't sure if you figured it out or not.

"I walked over to the office building and stood right outside the door. I was just a few feet from him when he came out. He looked straight at me and smiled. Kathryn, it was so surreal. I was looking into the face of my biological father, but he had no idea who I was. When he turned away from me, I got so emotional I had to leave. I drove around for a while until I calmed down."

Kate sighed and sat back down. "Where are you now?"

"I'm back at home with my parents."

"Do they know you were there?"

"Yes, of course. I told them everything. They understand why I did it, but they don't think it was a good idea."

"Well, get some rest. I'll call you tomorrow. Maybe by then the police will have more information."

Kate clicked the phone off and sat back on the couch.

Seconds later, the phone rang again. She jumped again.

"Hey, Kathryn. It's Mike Strickland."

"Mike, how are you? And how is Representative Hodges?"

"I'm fine, and Hodges is resting comfortably. How about you? Is your arm all right? And the bump on your head?"

"A little sore, but no damage done."

"Listen, Kathryn. I'd like to make amends for pushing you down into the dirt today. I know I was pretty rough, but I didn't know what was going on. How about if I take you out to dinner?"

The idea of going out to dinner with Mike sounded great, but she wondered if he really wanted to be with her or just felt an obligation to offer it. "That's very kind of you, Mike, but you don't owe me anything. And, besides, don't you have to stay close to Representative Hodges?"

"Nah, he's gonna be fine. He's slightly medicated and the doctors expect him to sleep through the night. To tell the truth, it's been a tough day for us all, and I could use a nice, quiet meal with somebody who looks a lot better than Jeremy Dodd."

She laughed. "Okay. I guess if you put it like that. I could meet you someplace."

"No, I'll pick you up. Do you have any suggestions for a hideaway where a renegade from a political campaign can eat without being recognized? After being on TV this afternoon, I've already had some people calling me."

Kate mentally clicked through the restaurants she knew. "There's a small home-cooking kind of place just outside of town. It isn't fancy, but the food is good and it's pretty secluded."

"Sounds perfect. Give me your address and I'll pick you up at six."

After she hung up, Kate wondered if she should be going to dinner with him. After all, he worked for the monster Hodges.

But Mike probably doesn't know anything about my mother. And he did protect me today at the rally when he covered my body with his own. That has to count for something. Besides, I might be able to learn more about Robert Hodges.

When Mike arrived, Kate invited him in and offered him a glass of wine, which he gladly accepted.

"Let me see that bump on your head." He put his wine glass down and held her face in his hands. "You look pretty good for a young lady who was shoved into the mud."

It was surprisingly tender, the way he touched the corner of her mouth with his thumb. "Better take care of that cut on your lip."

His hands were soft. *The hands of someone who works in an office.* "It's not so bad. I've had worse bumps and bruises before. But that reminds me." She left the room and returned with Mike's freshly laundered handkerchief. "Thanks for this. It really came in handy."

"No problem. If you're ever in need of a handkerchief, I'm your man." He grinned as he shoved it into his pocket.

As they drove to the restaurant, Mike filled her in on the details of the day. The police still had no idea who had fired the shot, but they had found some evidence inside the building that might help in locating the shooter. "Probably some whacko who blames all his problems on the current political climate. Bob was just the person he picked to take it out on."

"What's going to happen to the campaign?"

"The doctors tell us that Bob should be able to resume his schedule in a day or two."

"Don't you think this will affect his attitude toward campaigning in public?" she asked.

"Nah. Bob's a tough old bird and thrives on the campaign trail. You saw the way he looked up on that stage. That's his world. There's no way he could be deterred by a little thing like taking a bullet in the arm."

When they arrived at the restaurant, they put the awful events of the day aside and concentrated on friendly conversation. Mike was funny and pleasant to be with. She could see why Hodges would want him to engage with his major supporters.

He regaled her with stories about growing up on a farm in Iowa, milking cows at dawn, plowing fields, and baling hay. "It wasn't a hard decision for me. The first time I saw a hog slaughtered, I knew I didn't want to be a farmer. Going to law school was so much easier."

Kate tried to change the conversation to talk about Hodges or Liz Howley. "Tell me about the rest of the staff. What are they like?"

"Nothing special. Just the usual obsessive-compulsives," he grinned, then changed the subject back to her. He asked her about her background, where and when she was born, and what her interests were when she was growing up. He wanted to know all about her parents and their life in Bellevue.

She found that she talked about herself more than she ever had, and by the time he took her home, she felt she had known him for a long time.

But she still didn't know anything more about Robert Hodges.

As he walked her to the door of her house, she said, "Are you going to check on Hodges tonight?"

"Yeah, I'm going over to the hospital now. I'm sure everything is fine, but I'd like to see for myself before I head back to the hotel."

"Please give him my regards. And thank you for the dinner and the evening."

"I'm the one who has to thank you, Kathryn. You turned a really bad day into a really good evening. I sure hope you're going to decide to work with us." He gave her that same alluring smile she had seen at the campaign headquarters and touched his thumb to the corner of her mouth again. "Better not take a chance on opening an old wound," he said. He kissed her on the cheek and left.

Opening an old wound? Did that have a double meaning?

CHAPTER 31

Sunday

"Good morning, Kathryn. John Kaplan here."

The phone had awakened her, and she squinted at the clock. Seven o'clock.

"Mr. Kaplan?" *Why was he calling so early on Sunday morning?*

"I'm sorry to call you on the weekend, but something's come up that I need to talk to you about. Can you to come to my office today? Would nine o'clock work?"

"I can be there at nine. But what's this about, Mr. Kaplan?"

"We may have a clue to your parents' deaths."

* * *

"How is Hodges doing?" a reporter shouted as Mike Strickland made his way into Bellevue Hospital early Sunday morning. He had approached a side door, hoping to find a way in that wasn't surrounded by reporters, but they were covering every entrance.

Mike didn't stop but slowed his pace enough to respond to a few questions. "He's fine. I just talked to him on the phone and he says he's feeling great."

"Do you know when he'll be released?"

"We'll talk to the doctors about that this morning."

"What kind of mood is he in? Is he ready to return to the campaign trail?"

"He's rarin' to go. It's all I can do to keep him tied down until the hospital gives him the all-clear."

The last comment brought a round of laughter from the press corps as he eased past the group and entered through the revolving door. He didn't want them to know the concern he felt when he had phoned the hospital earlier. Hodges said he felt good, but his speech was slow, as if he wasn't thinking clearly. Quite a change from his usual energetic, forceful personality.

Several police lined the hallways, and two officers stationed themselves outside Hodges's hospital room. Mike showed them his campaign ID badge, and they let him into the room.

Flowers were everywhere, on the table tops, in corners, even in the bathroom.

Jeremy and Elizabeth were already there. Liz was seated in a chair next to the bed, her ever-present laptop resting on her knees. When she looked up, he noticed dark circles under her eyes. *I wonder if she got any sleep last night.*

Jeremy stood at the foot of the bed reading out loud from the green schedule sheet. Hodges was propped up in bed, his right shoulder bandaged and an IV going into the vein of his left arm. He beamed when he saw Mike.

"Well, look who's here. Glad you could make some time in your busy schedule to join us for staff meeting."

Mike grinned. Maybe it wasn't so bad after all. "I was hoping to get a little time off due to the circumstances, but it looks like I'm out of luck." He patted Liz's shoulder as he moved past her and over to the bed to talk to Hodges.

"You're looking pretty good. They must have some super meds around here. Maybe I should check myself in for a day or two."

"I highly recommend it," responded Hodges. "Best night's sleep I've had in years. And the hospital staff has been great. Liz, don't forget to send a thank-you card to the staff on this floor. And make sure they distribute all these flowers to other patients."

"Will do. I've asked Jennie to take over the job of responding to the well-wishes that are coming in through the website. We're getting phone calls and emails from all over the country. It's going to take a while to answer all of them."

"Just make sure we thank every single one of them." Hodges turned back to Mike. "The president even called me this morning. I guess that's one way to get his attention. Maybe he'll be willing to bend a little on that technology bill."

Mike laughed. "Don't count on it. He's a pretty tough cookie. On the other hand . . ."

Jeremy pumped his fist in the air. "This is going to seal the election for us. I wouldn't be surprised if the Gray Man concedes the race right now."

Mike ignored the interruption and turned his back to Jeremy. "Do you know when they plan to release you?"

"They want to keep me for another night, just to make sure, and release me tomorrow. From my point of view, I'd be happy to leave right now. I feel great and sitting around in this bed for another day isn't too appealing to me. But I'll do whatever they say."

Jeremy clicked his ball point pen several times excitedly. "This'll make a great story. The doctors want you to stay for another day, but you're trying to talk them into letting you go. The public will love it. I'll feed this to the press when I leave." He had a broad smile on his face as he started jotting down notes, apparently aware that the shooting was going to work in his candidate's favor. Yesterday, he had worried that Hodges had been knocked out of the race, but today he could see that the campaign was actually going to benefit from the assassination attempt. He looked positively gleeful.

"Drop it, Jeremy." Mike glared at the campaign manager. "This isn't about the campaign. We almost lost Bob yesterday, and you're trying to turn this into some kind of promotion. Just let the press know the facts without your usual spin."

Jeremy scowled in response. "Back off, Strict Man. I don't need you to tell me how to do my job. I'm going to give this campaign every advantage I can, and, if it means using this to persuade voters of Bob's energy and determination, that's what I'm going to do."

Mike bit back the retort that came to mind. He knew he couldn't get into a shouting match in this hospital room with his candidate lying injured in the bed and police stationed just outside the door.

Elizabeth closed her laptop and stood. "This is not the time or place to have this conversation. Jeremy and I have to go, anyway. He'll brief the press, and I'll go back to the hotel and start contacting folks about the meetings we have to cancel. Bob, I'll drop by again this afternoon. In the meantime, call me if you need anything." She turned to Mike and Jeremy. "Let's go now so Bob can get some rest."

"Mike, I'd like you to stay for a few minutes," Hodges said. "Jeremy, thanks for all the work you're doing on the campaign. Liz, let me know if any of the cancellations are a problem. We can talk about rescheduling later. I'm really depending on the two of you to handle this with your usual professionalism."

"No problem, boss," Jeremy said. "We'll see you later this afternoon." He shot a dark look at Mike before he and Elizabeth left the room.

CHAPTER 32

M ike sank down in the chair Elizabeth had vacated.
"You were pretty hard on Jeremy, Mike. Anything bothering you?"

"No. I just get annoyed with him constantly working the angles. You don't need to run for office that way. Your record and positions speak for themselves. I think some voters are actually turned off by the way he's handling this campaign."

"I'll speak to him about it. I know he's got some rough edges, but he's doing everything he can to make sure we win, so don't be too hard on him."

"Yeah, okay. I guess I'm just tired. I was out late last night."
"Oh?"

Mike massaged his temples, trying to rub the fatigue and frustration away. "I took Kathryn Frasier out to dinner. She and I had been standing next to each other in the audience at the rally. When the gun was fired, I pushed her down to the ground. It hurt her arm and she got a bump on her head, but she was a good sport about it, so I asked her to dinner last night."

"I'm glad you had a chance to take her out. She seems like a fine young woman." Hodges picked up a cup of water from the bedside table, took a long sip, and put it back. "Did you get any information about her background?"

"Yeah. She told me pretty much everything about herself. Good parents, good upbringing, good education. A real princess story, except that her parents died in a car accident a few months ago."

"Did you find out how old she is?"
"She's twenty-seven."

There was a prolonged silence while Hodges gazed at the IV bag that was dripping life-sustaining fluids into his body.

Mike looked at his friend closely. This was a Hodges he didn't know. The man he knew was dynamic, in charge of his own destiny, enjoying the ups and downs of the political stage. *Why is he so distracted by Kathryn Frasier?*

Mike finally spoke up. "Bob, you and I have been friends a long time. I've always felt we could be frank with each other, but now it seems like there's something you're not telling me. I can't help you if you don't let me in on it."

Hodges leaned back on his pillow and shifted his body to gaze at the aspen tree just outside the window. His voice took on a quiet, confidential tone. "You know, Mike, I've spent my whole life looking forward. The next campaign, the next bill before congress, the next fundraiser. It was all about rushing ahead to do as much as I could." He looked over at his colleague.

"Yesterday, when the bullet hit me, I thought I was facing the end. They say your life plays out before your eyes when you get close to death, but I didn't see any of my accomplishments. I saw the things that hadn't yet been done.

"Last night, as I lay in this bed, I determined I would redouble my efforts to help the people of this state and the country. There's more to do, and I think I can accomplish a lot as governor." He made a fist with his left hand and firmly planted it on the bed. "I want to win this race now more than ever."

Mike's pulse beat in time with Hodges's determination. This was the candidate he had tied his own future to. The statesman whose ideals pushed him into service. "That's great, Bob. I'll be with you all the way."

"Thanks. And Mike, I need you to do another favor for me. But it has to be done in secret."

CHAPTER 33

When Kate arrived at Kaplan's office, she found him talking to another man, one she had seen on TV.

"Kathryn, thank you for coming. Have you met Police Commissioner Blake?"

Gerald Blake was short and slim. With his white hair, bright blue eyes, and rosy cheeks, he looked more like a kindly grandfather than a senior law enforcement officer. He stood and extended his hand. "Kathryn, so nice to meet you." He had a firm handshake and a soft, confident voice with a distinct drawl. *A real Southern gentleman*, she thought.

"Please have a seat, Kathryn," Mr. Kaplan said. The two men remained standing while Kate settled into one of the straight chairs. "The commissioner and I were just talking about the events at the rally yesterday. Something came up that you might be able to help us with."

"Me? I can't imagine how I can help, but I'll do anything I can."

"Gerald, why don't you tell Kathryn what you discovered."

"Yes, of course." Blake moved so that he was standing directly in front of Kate. "You see, Kathryn, the police confiscated a number of videos that were taken at the rally at the time of the shooting. We spent several hours last night reviewing them, and they show clearly that Hodges was standing at the podium and suddenly leaned over to his right side to reach out to a baby that someone was holding up." Blake bent over and extended his right arm to illustrate the position. "The shot was fired just as he stretched out his arm, and the bullet hit him just about here." Blake pointed to the area just above his armpit. "If he hadn't moved so quickly, he wouldn't have been hit." He stood upright and pointed to indicate the path of the bullet if Hodges hadn't been in the way. "The bullet would have struck the man sitting just behind him on the stage. That man was Dean Jefferson."

Kate's mouth dropped open. "Dean Jefferson? The dean of engineering?"

"Exactly. Now, this is just a hunch. Suppose the shooter wasn't trying to hit Representative Hodges at all but was aiming for Dean Jefferson. We've seen disenchanted students attack and sometimes even kill, professors they think did them wrong."

He gestured toward Kaplan. "When I told John about this theory, he immediately let me know there was some suspicion about your own parents' deaths. Since your father had once taught in the School of Engineering, we wondered if a student who was mad at Dean Jefferson could also have been resentful of your father."

"Angry enough to kill?"

Blake leaned back against the desk and crossed his arms over his chest. "It's possible. Do you know if anyone at the university ever threatened your dad?"

"No, not at all. I'm sure I would remember something like that."

"Can you think of anyone who may have held a grudge? Maybe because of a bad class grade or failing an oral exam? Anyone at all?"

Kate stared at the floor while she mentally ticked through the students she had known. "I don't know any student who held a grudge against my father. Dad hadn't been at the university for several years, and I remember him saying all his graduate students had finished their studies before he left."

"It could even be someone from a long time ago. We know of cases where people held resentment in for years, but then something triggered them to take action against their perceived enemy."

"I know my father gave students failing grades when they deserved them, but I never heard him say anything about anyone being angry at him personally."

"Well, keep it in mind," Blake said as he handed her a card with his phone information. "Contact me directly if you think of anything. I'll also keep you informed if we get a break in the ID of the shooter.

"If our theory is correct and it is a disgruntled student, I expect we'll find him or her very soon. In the meantime, the Secret Service is providing coverage for Hodges, and we've put a protective detail at Dean Jefferson's home."

* * *

Kate called Cece as soon as she got home. "I think we've been barking up the wrong tree."

"What do you mean?"

Kate described the meeting with Mr. Kaplan and Commissioner Blake. "We've been concentrating on Representative Hodges as someone who may have had something to do with my folks' accident. But if the shooter at the rally was an engineering student who had a grudge against professors, he or she might have wanted to target my dad too. It would be easy for a student to convince my father to meet them for dinner since he always loved to hear how his students were doing. On the other hand, Dad had zero interest in politics."

"If it was a student, do you have any idea who it could be?"

"No. I knew some of Dad's students, but not all of them. Commissioner Blake seems to think they can track down the shooter pretty quickly, so we should know something soon. In the meantime, we can forget about Robert Hodges."

CHAPTER 34

When Mike arrived back at his hotel, he found members of the press lounging in the hotel lobby, waiting for him, and he spent several minutes filling them in on Representative Hodges's condition. When he got to his room, he ordered a sandwich from room service and sat on the side of the bed, lost in thought about the task that Hodges had asked him to help with.

Before he finished eating, Hodges called. "Mike, I need you to come back to the hospital right away. Something's come up that you should be aware of. See if you can get in touch with Jeremy and Elizabeth. They need to be here too."

"No problem. Be there in a few."

Actually, it was a problem. Mike was exhausted, drained from the events of the past twenty-four hours. All he wanted to do was go to sleep and forget all the nonsense of the political world for a few hours. But Hodges wouldn't ask him to come unless it was important. He called Elizabeth and told her to get to the hospital and to bring Jeremy with her.

When Mike entered the hospital room, Hodges was talking quietly with Police Commissioner Blake.

"Mike, thanks for coming back on such short notice. You remember Commissioner Blake."

"Yes, of course," Mike said as he shook hands with the commissioner. "We met at the news conference after the shooting."

"Good to see you again, Mike," Blake drawled, "although I'm sorry it's under these circumstances."

Within a couple of minutes, Elizabeth and Jeremy came in.

Jeremy was beaming. News of the shooting had turned the tide and given new life to the campaign. It seemed that everyone in the state had suddenly become supportive of Robert Hodges for governor. Big donors were tripping over themselves to get on board, and Jeremy was riding the wave.

Hodges told the team that Commissioner Blake had new information in the case. Jeremy's eyes lit up. Mike could almost see him preparing another headline story for the evening news. Hodges gestured toward Blake. "Commissioner, please tell my staff what you've found."

Blake took a roll of Life Savers out of his pocket and popped one in his mouth. "As Representative Hodges said, we've uncovered some new information in the case, and we wanted to report it to you first. There'll be a press conference outside the hospital immediately after this meeting to present our findings to the public. We'd like for one of you to be the spokesperson for Representative Hodges at the news conference, if possible."

Hodges spoke up. "Mike will represent me."

"Fine." Blake continued, "Now let me tell you our current theory. After a thorough investigation of the videos taken at the rally, we've concluded that the intended victim of the shooting may not have been Representative Hodges but could have been Dean Jefferson of the School of Engineering at the university."

"What?" Jeremy sounded incredulous. "That's ridiculous. Representative Hodges was the one who was shot."

I guess this is going to destroy his whole narrative of Hodges as the intended assassination victim, thought Mike. *He'll have to come up with another story for the press.*

Blake looked at Jeremy and shrugged his shoulders. "It's our job to follow the evidence. Once we determined where the shot originated, we were able to pin down the exact location. It was on the third floor, corner storage room. The window in that room was unlocked. It only took us a little while to find the gun. It had been stashed above a section of the drop ceiling. It was a stolen gun, and it had been wiped clean, so it's not much help.

"But surveillance video shows a young man leaving the building right after the shooting that we haven't been able to account for. He's been identified as . . ." He paused and pulled a slip of paper from his jacket pocket. "Clark Bellingham, an engineering graduate student at the university. We checked with Dean Jefferson and he told us that he had warned Bellingham a month or so ago about his poor performance. He said the guy got very angry when he was told he might get kicked out of school if he didn't improve." Blake folded the paper and put it back in his pocket.

"We haven't been able to locate Bellingham yet, but we will. We have an APB out on him, and we're checking with his family in Oklahoma to see if they know his whereabouts. I'll spare you the rest of the details, but I wanted you to know the latest developments."

Mike could see the gears turning in Jeremy's head as he started to construct a new story that would make Hodges look like a hero.

"Needless to say, I'm very relieved to hear this news," Hodges said. "Commissioner, please give our thanks to the fine folks in the Bellevue Police Department for their quick work. Mike, I'd like you to go downstairs with Blake and make a statement on my behalf. Let everyone know we're happy to hear the police have a suspect, and we'll provide any assistance we can as the investigation moves forward."

The Commissioner put his hand on Hodges's good shoulder. "Glad you didn't lean any further over to pick up that baby. Could have been a real tragedy." He patted him gently. "Hope you get over that injury real soon." He motioned for Mike to follow him outside

As Mike got to the door of the room, he looked back to see Jeremy furiously scribbling on his notepad.

CHAPTER 35

The weather Sunday afternoon was still beautiful, and Kate spent an hour on the trails at Campbell Park with Barkley at her side. The puzzle pieces galloped around in her head like multicolored horses on a carousel. *The automobile accident, Phil Warren, Mike Strickland, Cece, the Goldmans, Representative Hodges, Mr. Kaplan, Commissioner Blake, Tommy, Gavin, the shooting, engineering students.*

But nothing fit together. Were they all related or just random people and events? Like the horses, they just went round and round and didn't get anywhere.

And what about the latest clue? *Check the flower box.* What could it mean?

She usually felt energized after a run, but today she was exhausted. Her arm still hurt and her mind seemed fuzzy. *You're overthinking everything. Let it go. Stop trying to analyze every detail.*

She showered and dressed to attend the afternoon service at her church. She sat in a pew in the back of the small sanctuary and tried to concentrate. The title of the sermon printed in the bulletin was "Stress Less." *He must have prepared this message just for me,* she thought. *Just what I need.*

Reverend Whitefield took to the pulpit and began, "Our Scripture lesson this afternoon is from the book of Matthew, chapter 6." He opened his Bible to the passage and continued. "Consider the lilies of the field, how they grow: they neither toil nor spin, yet I tell you, even Solomon in all his glory was not arrayed like one of these. But if God so clothes the grass of the field, which today is alive and tomorrow is thrown into the oven, will he not much more clothe you, O you of little faith?"

Lilies of the field.

Reverend Whitefield went on, "Here in Bellevue, we are surrounded by magnificent vistas of mountains, forests, and lakes. If you've ever walked past a field of flowers in bloom waving against the green grass, you can't help but be in awe of God's creation."

A field of flowers in bloom.

"But Bellevue is also a community of high achievers, people who are used to winning, and that can produce a great deal of stress. We need to step back and realize that God provides for us as He provides for the flowers of the field . . ."

Flowers of the field. Check the flower box. So much for taking her mind off the latest clue.

When she returned home, Kate caught the evening news and saw Commissioner Blake's press conference where he identified an engineering graduate student named Clark Bellingham as a person of interest in the shooting. *So, it was a grad student after all. Did Clark Bellingham know Dad?*

There was a picture of Bellingham on the screen. He had a thick mop of light-colored hair, and there was something odd about his face. It was asymmetrical. One eye drooped a little below the other one. Kate searched her memory but couldn't remember ever having seen him before. *I'm sure I'd remember that face if I'd seen it.*

The phone rang just after the evening newscast. It was Tommy Abrahams.

"Kathryn, did you see the news this evening? They think an engineering student may have been the shooter at the rally on Saturday." Tommy had taken technical classes at the university and knew many of the students.

"Yes. I learned about it this morning. Do you know Clark Bellingham?"

Tommy's voice was shrill and shaky. "Yes, I was in a couple of classes with him. And he lives in the same apartment building I do."

Kate had been lying back on the couch, but now she bolted upright. "Do you know him well?"

"Not really. I just know him to say hello, that sort of thing."

"Do you think he's mentally unstable? Would he be capable of shooting someone?"

"Gosh, Kathryn, I don't know. He's a little strange, but so are a lot of graduate students. I heard he had some pretty radical political views, but I never talked to him about any of it. But you said you heard about him this morning. How did you find out so early?"

"My family's lawyer called me this morning. He thought that an engineering student might have been targeting professors. Since my dad was once a professor in engineering, my lawyer had the idea this student might have had something to do with my parents' automobile accident."

There was a long silence. When Tommy spoke again, his voice was almost a whisper. "Somebody thinks your parents were murdered?"

How stupid of me. Kate realized that she had said too much, especially to a sensitive person like Tommy. She made her voice sound calm and reassuring. "It was just a theory somebody had. There's no real evidence. I'm sure it's nothing."

After their conversation ended, Kate heated a can of soup and made herself a sandwich. Before she finished eating, her phone rang again.

"Kathryn, John Kaplan here. I have some news I need to share with you."

Kate put her sandwich down and braced herself. He wouldn't call unless it was important. "What is it, Mr. Kaplan?"

"You've probably heard that the police are looking for an engineering grad student named Clark Bellingham."

"Yes, I just saw it on the news."

"When they identified him, they had some folks at the university take a look at Bellingham's record. They discovered that he was a student in one of your father's engineering classes when he was an undergraduate." Kaplan spoke slowly and quietly. "Your father gave him a failing grade."

Kate gulped. "So, you think Clark Bellingham is a possible suspect in my parents' deaths?"

"There's no way to know, but we need to be alert to any possibility. I'm sure the police will find him soon, but I wanted to contact you to let you know this information. And, one other thing, Kathryn. You need to be on your guard. There's no telling what he might do."

"But there's no reason I would be in danger. I haven't done anything to him."

"That's true, Kathryn. But people do strange things when they're being hunted by the police. Just make sure your doors and windows are all locked and your alarm system is armed. I'm sure it's nothing, but we don't want you taking any chances."

"Thanks, Mr. Kaplan. I'll check everything. Good night."

After she hung up, Kate checked every door and window. She got out the flashlight and put it on her bedside table. She made sure her phone was fully charged and her alarm system was on. And she gave Barkley the special treat of sleeping on the foot of her bed. She did not sleep soundly.

CHAPTER 36

Monday

"The police consider this man to be armed and dangerous. If you see him or have any information of his whereabouts, you should contact the authorities immediately."

Kate thought the anchorman seemed to be talking directly to her as she watched the TV newscast from her bed on Monday morning. The lead story was all about the shooting and the hunt for Clark Bellingham. The police had issued an all-points bulletin but hadn't located him yet. Kate stared at the picture of Bellingham on the screen and felt a drop of sweat trickle down her neck.

John Kaplan called to give her an update on the situation. "The police searched Bellingham's apartment and found some pretty interesting political documents. If he did the shooting, he could have had issues with Representative Hodges as well as Dean Jefferson. The police are working hard but haven't come up with a solid lead on his whereabouts yet."

"Can the police check where he was the weekend my parents died?" Kate asked.

"I don't know, but I'll ask Commissioner Blake about it. He's promised to keep me up to date, and I'll let you know if I find out anything."

Kate thanked him for the information and leaned back against the pillows on her bed. Figuring out what had happened at the rally was a lot more complicated than solving a math problem or building a computer system.

Cece, forgive me, she thought, as she considered how quickly she had become suspicious of her sister. *But how can you tell what's real and what's just perception? Cece herself taught me that things are often not what they seem. Am I going to go through life suspecting bad motives from the people I know?*

As she poured a bowl of cereal for breakfast, the doorbell rang. Now what? It was a florist delivery. She took the flowers into the house and opened the card. Inside was a note and a handkerchief with the initials MS. The note said, "Enjoyed the dinner. Maybe you should keep this in case of emergencies. Mike."

Kate breathed in the fragrant aroma of the flowers and smiled at the cute reference to the handkerchief. *Very charming.* She put the vase filled with daisies and small pink carnations on her dining room table. Feathery ferns filled out the arrangement.

She brought her cereal and coffee to the dining room, sat down, and opened the online version of the local newspaper. There was a picture of Mike Strickland standing behind Commissioner Blake at the news conference, and a smaller picture of Clark Bellingham.

She stared at the picture of Mike. Standing with his arms folded across his chest and a serious frown on his face, he seemed the very picture of the professional chief of staff completely in charge of the situation. He was so handsome and so smooth.

Dinner with him had been great, but did his charm have a purpose to it? She hadn't gotten any information about Hodges from him, but he had learned a lot about her. He certainly had made her feel like she was the only person in the room, just like Tommy said. That was his job when he met with big donors, but there was no reason he would need to be especially charming with her. *Or was there?*

Still, it was nice of him to send the flowers, she thought as she admired the bouquet sitting in the center of the table. Daisies on a field of green ferns.

As she stood to take her dishes to the kitchen, it hit her. "Oh, how stupid of me," she said out loud as she put the dishes down and slapped the side of her head with the heel of her hand. "Check the flower box!" She grabbed her phone and called. "Cece, can you come over? I think I just found a piece of the puzzle."

* * *

"I'm so excited. What did you find?" Cece arrived looking flushed.

"It finally dawned on me." Kate pointed to the box she had brought out and placed on the dining room table. It had a soft fabric covering in a floral pattern—white daisies on a green background.

"The flower box!" Cece threw her hands in the air and hugged Kathryn.

"Maybe. This is the box that I used to put things in, special things, when I was a child. I had stashed it away in the back of a cabinet in my bedroom and forgot all about it. Dad must have put something in there, something he wanted me to find."

"Have you looked in it yet?"

"No, I wanted to wait for you."

They stared at the box for a minute, as if afraid to look inside.

Kate opened the lid slowly, as if she expected something to jump out at her. Inside were a lot of papers and cards, some of them turning yellow with age.

The girls removed the contents, one item at a time. There were two poems that Kate had written in elementary school and a small notebook where she had copied favorite quotes. A tiny plastic bag contained the first baby tooth she had lost. Cece wrinkled her nose and offered up her surprise that a smart person like

Kate would keep such a thing. "Sentimentality must be universal," she said.

They found coins and stamps from various places, a few school papers and several cards from her parents. There was a bracelet she had worn in kindergarten and a picture she had drawn of her family when she was seven years old.

The two girls examined each item carefully, enjoying the memories and looking for clues to their puzzle. As they got to the bottom, the only remaining thing was an envelope labeled "first lock."

"This is the first lock of hair they cut when I was a baby," Kate said as she handed the envelope to Cece. "I'm disappointed. I thought we would find something in here, but that's all there is."

Cece opened the envelope and took out the lock of brown hair that was tied with two pink ribbons, one wide and the other narrow. "Your hair was lighter then," she said.

"Yeah. I guess it's gotten darker over time." Kate continued sifting through the papers and cards on the table.

"My parents saved my first lock of hair too," Cece said. "I guess it's what all parents do. They only tied mine up with one ribbon, though. You must be extra special since you got two ribbons."

Kate looked up and frowned. "What two ribbons?"

Cece held up the lock of baby hair with the two pink ribbons, and Kate took it from her. "Aha," she said as she delicately examined each of the ribbons. On the underside of the wider ribbon, written in white ink, were the words "Find a key unlike all the other keys."

CHAPTER 37

"**E**ureka," Cece exclaimed in a whisper. "Do you suppose that's the clue?"

"You bet it is. Only my father would come up with something like that." Kate carefully untied the ribbon and examined it.

"How clever to put a clue about a key on a ribbon around a lock," Cece giggled. "I'm astounded by your father's genius. But what does it mean?"

"That's the question. What kind of key would be unlike all the others?"

They spent the next hour looking through drawers and cabinets to find all the keys that Kate had in her house. Door keys, desk keys, filing cabinet keys, even keys that couldn't be identified. The most unconventional one was Kate's car key, which was considerably larger than the rest. They unlocked her car and went through it, looking for anything unusual. They checked the trunk and the glove compartment. Nothing.

Kate laid her car key on the kitchen table and dropped into one of the chairs. This mass search wasn't turning up anything. It had to be something more subtle.

"Suppose it's not a real key," she said. "Maybe Dad had something else in mind."

Cece helped herself to a glass of water from the sink. "What else could it be?" she asked.

"Maybe it's something like 'the key to happiness' or 'the key to success.' "

"That's pretty deep stuff. Did he ever talk to you about any of those things? You know, the usual parent-child serious talk?"

"We had plenty of serious talks, but I don't remember him ever saying anything in exactly that way. Maybe we should look in the envelope again. I think we're missing something."

But there was nothing else in the envelope. They had the entirety of the clue, but they were clueless.

Kate shook the empty box, hoping something would fall out and give them further information, but, like the pantry of the widow of Zarephath, it had yielded its singular treasure. The box was empty. The girls returned all the papers, cards, and special items to the box. In the end, they had only the pink ribbon with its cryptic clue.

"Back to the drawing board," Kate said as she closed the cover on the box. "Looks like we have another conundrum that we need to chew on for a while."

Cece put her glass in the sink and checked her watch. "I have to leave in a few minutes. The local theater company is performing an original production, and I'm trying out for a part in the play. Auditions are this afternoon."

"Cece, that's so exciting. I'm thrilled for you. What's the play?"

"It's called *Bellevue Revealed*. It's a satirical look at the so-called perfect town of Bellevue." She pulled a flyer out of her purse and gave it to Kate. "Here's the blurb they're going to put on the advertising posters."

Beautiful Bellevue. What could be wrong with a bunch of techno-whizzes all cozied up in one town, unaffected by the plights of the world, thinking their exclusive utopia is the product of their own collective genius? Nothing. It just makes things all the more interesting when reality drops in to set things straight.

Kate laughed out loud at the idea of a play tweaking the good people of the ego-driven town of Bellevue. "This sounds hilarious. I hope you get a part," she said as she handed the flyer back to Cece.

"My audition should be over by about five o'clock. Why don't we meet somewhere for an early dinner and mull over this new clue?"

"That'd be great. Do you know where Cafe Rouge is? It's a beautiful day and they have outdoor dining. We could meet there."

"Cafe Rouge it is. I'll see you there around five-thirty."

After Cece left, Kate found her phone and sent a text to Mike. THANK YOU FOR THE FLOWERS. THEY'RE BEAUTIFUL!

A few minutes later, she got a response. MY PLEASURE. I'M OUT OF TOWN RIGHT NOW, BUT I LEFT SOMETHING FOR YOU AT HODGES'S CAMPAIGN HEADQUARTERS. THERE'S AN ENVELOPE ON HIS DESK WITH YOUR NAME ON IT. STOP BY AND PICK IT UP WHEN YOU GET A CHANCE. MS.

Something for me?

* * *

Kate found a sign on the door to the campaign office. "Staff and volunteers: We will be closed for the next couple of days. Please return for our regular hours on Wednesday."

They must be trying to get themselves reorganized after the shooting. The door was unlocked, though, so Kate pushed it open and entered the large outer room. She heard voices coming from the office Jeremy Dodd had been using.

"This could be a problem, Liz," the man said. "If Grayson gets onto it, we'll be in trouble. We need to do something."

"Don't worry, Jeremy. I know how to handle this. Remember, I've been there before."

Kate felt like she was eavesdropping. *Not nice. On the other hand, maybe I can learn something.* She took another step into the room.

The outer door opened behind her, and a loud sneeze startled her. She whirled around and found a campaign staff member wiping his nose on the back of his hand. He shook his head at her. "This place is so dusty. Always gets to my allergies."

Elizabeth Howley appeared at the door of the office where she had been arguing with Jeremy Dodd. She had a grim expression on her face. "What are you two doing here?"

The staff member took a handkerchief out of his pocket and wiped his nose again. "I left my jacket here before the rally, and I just stopped by to pick it up." He walked over to a side area and retrieved a blue windbreaker. "See ya, Ms. Howley," he said, nodding to Liz. As he walked past Kate, he gave her a knowing look, as if to say, "Be careful. The lioness is unleashed."

Liz cast an icy stare at Kate. "How long have you been standing there? Didn't you see the sign on the door?"

Wouldn't you like to know how long I've been standing here?

"Mike Strickland left an envelope for me on Representative Hodges's desk. It has my name on it. Kathryn Frasier."

"I know who you are. Wait here. I'll check." Elizabeth went into Hodges's office and returned holding an envelope. She handed it to Kate and opened the outer door, motioning for her to leave.

"Thanks for your help." *And for your warm hospitality.*

As she exited the building, Kate heard the lock turn on the door behind her.

When she got to her car, she opened the envelope. Inside was a handwritten note that said, "You are invited to Governor Hodges's inauguration (if we win) as my date. You can RSVP on election night. Mike."

Funny. She texted him. JUST PICKED UP THE ENVELOPE. VERY CUTE.

In a few seconds, her phone rang. "So, what do you think?" Mike said. "Are you up for a gubernatorial inauguration?"

"I'll let you know on election night."

"Fair enough. By the way, I'm just over in Barton, and I'm coming back through Bellevue to take some potential donors to dinner tonight. Would you like to join me?"

"I can't, Mike. I promised a friend I'd meet her for dinner at Cafe Rouge tonight. Maybe another time."

"Okay. Have a good evening."

When Kate returned home, she caught the afternoon news at five o'clock. Lead story: Clark Bellingham was still at large.

CHAPTER 38

K ate parked her car in the corner lot and strolled down the sidewalk toward Cafe Rouge. Worries about Clark Bellingham faded as she wrapped her mind around the latest clue.

A key unlike all the other keys. This was the third clue, and her father always left three or four. Maybe this was the final one. And if the Goldmans were right, it might unlock the mystery of what happened to her parents.

As she walked past the outdoor tables with their blue-and-white scalloped umbrellas, a familiar voice called out, "Hey, Kathryn."

She turned to see Phil Warren sitting at one of the outside tables. A woman sat next to him and a bottle of wine was open on the table. A few books and papers were scattered in front of them. This couldn't have been the woman she saw him embrace at the car repair shop because this one was a redhead. *I can see I was right about him. This guy must have a woman on every corner.*

Phil walked around the table toward her and she felt her knees go wobbly. She wanted to believe all those things her father had said about him. Solid to the core. Honorable. Trustworthy. Hardly the playboy she was seeing.

He had an "I know something you don't know" smile on his face as he extended his hand to her. The same smile he had used a few days before at the car shop.

Armed with the evidence of his womanizing, she pulled herself up as straight and tall as she could and returned his gaze openly, some might even think defiantly, as if to say, "You cannot beguile me." But she couldn't resist smiling back.

"Hello, Phil," she said as she took his hand. It was the first time Kate could remember that she had used his given name. And the first time she had touched him.

His handshake was strong and hard, and she returned it with a firmness of her own. It seemed to Kate that he held her hand just a second or two longer than was called for. "Come meet Emily."

There was no graceful way out of this situation, so she followed him to the small round table on the veranda. "Emily Smithson, this is Kathryn Frasier. Kathryn is one of my customers."

The two women exchanged hellos, and Phil pulled out a chair. "Please join us."

"No, thank you. I don't want to intrude. I'm meeting a friend for dinner. She should be here in a few minutes."

"Why don't you sit with us until she comes?" he asked.

"Yes, please join us," Emily said. She sounded sincere.

How can I refuse? Kate sat down at the table.

Phil signaled and a young waitress bounced up to the table and addressed Kate. "Hi. I'm Julie. Can I get you something?"

"No, thanks. I'm not staying."

"Another wine glass," Phil said.

I can't believe I'm the third wheel at a table with Phil and another woman.

Phil poured wine into Kate's glass. "Emily is my professor in classical Greek history. We were just going through some background material for a paper I'm writing on Aristotle."

His college professor? "You're taking a course in classical Greek history?"

"Yes. Surprised?"

"No. Well, maybe a little."

"There's more to life than oil changes, you know."

Emily gathered the papers strewn on the table and stacked them neatly into a folder. "I wish you'd come earlier. You could've met my husband. He just left to get the car. He's a history professor too, and we both have classes tonight, so I'll be leaving in a minute."

"Sorry I missed him." *All right, so Phil isn't seeing this woman. But what about the brunette at the auto shop?*

A gray Kia pulled up to the curb and beeped a couple of times. "There he is now." Emily waved toward the car. "Coming!" She pushed her folder into a canvas bag. "I'm looking forward to that paper, Phil. And Kathryn, I hope to see you again someday."

Phil helped Emily carry her books to the car, then returned to the table. He gazed at Kathryn in silence for a few seconds while he fingered the stem on his wine glass. "Why didn't you stop in to see me when you picked up your car last Friday? Maclean told me you'd been there."

Why didn't I stop in? Maybe because you were taking care of some personal business. And she didn't look like a college professor. "I was going to, but I saw you talking to someone, and I didn't want to interrupt."

Phil gave her a quizzical look. Then a smile of understanding slowly spread across his face. "You must have seen me talking to my sister, Molly."

"Your . . . sister?" The womanizing theory seemed to be falling apart.

"Yes. She's in town from college and dropped by to see me. I wish you'd come over. I'd like you to meet her."

They spent the next few minutes talking about Molly Warren, the college she was attending, and her interests and activities. Kate asked about her field of study.

"She's majoring in computer science," Phil responded.

"That's wonderful. That was my major."

"Really? What got you interested in computer science?"

Kate pushed a stray lock of hair behind her ear. "It was just a natural fit for me. I guess people who have an analytical mind-set gravitate toward subjects like engineering or computer science."

"That sounds a lot like Molly. She has a very logical way of thinking." Phil put his elbows on the table and leaned his chin into his hands. "What is it that you like so much about computers?"

"Computer programming is fun. You're creating something that's unique, and you're choosing how to build it. I guess it's a lot like architecture but without the bricks."

They both laughed at the comparison.

Kate took a sip of chianti. "How about you? Have you always been interested in history?"

He sat back in his chair and stretched his legs under the table. "No. I studied engineering in school, but I wanted to learn something about the Greeks. Aristotle is intriguing to me because he was not just a philosopher but was also considered the first real scientist. He looked at the world and tried to draw conclusions based on his observations, using an empirical model, much like modern scientists."

"My dad was a fan of Aristotle too. He even had a small bust of him on his desk. I have it in my house now. There was one quote of Aristotle's that he especially liked. Something about how we don't do good things because of our virtue, but we have virtue because we do good things. Dad used to say 'We are what we do.'"

"I know that quote. Aristotle had a lot of great lines." He picked up a small brown book from the table and flipped through its pages. "Here's a good one: 'Love is composed of a single soul inhabiting two bodies.' "

He looked up and smiled again, waiting for her to respond, but all she could think to say was, "That's interesting."

Is this the way he interacts with all women? She took another sip of wine.

A silver Mercedes pulled up to the curb across the street.

"That must be Gavin Connelly," Kate said. "He's the CEO of ArcTron Labs, where my father used to work."

"I know him. He sold us his old car when he bought the new one. It's a real beauty, isn't it?"

As Gavin crossed the street toward them, Phil stood and waved him over.

The newcomer reached across the short, wrought-iron fence that separated the patio from the sidewalk to shake hands with Phil. "Hi, Phil. Kathryn, good to see you again."

"How was your trip?" Kate asked. Then she turned to Phil. "Gavin spent the weekend in Reno."

"Oh, really? Were you over there on business?"

"No. Just a little getaway. But I'd never been there before, so I thought it'd be a good time to take the new car on the road. The weather was great, and I enjoyed the drive over and back."

"Sounds like fun," said Phil. "Why don't you join us?" He motioned for the waitress to bring another glass.

"Don't bring a glass for me," Gavin said. "I can't stay. I'm meeting someone at The Pointe Grill in a few minutes. One of the patent lawyers we keep in business. But it was good to see both of you." He gave a short wave as he walked away.

"Nice guy," said Phil as he took his seat. "Have you known him long?"

"Just since he took over as CEO of ArcTron. I guess that's been a couple of years. Have you known him for a long time?"

"I met him when he brought his old car in a couple of months ago. He just wanted us to buy it from him so he wouldn't have to worry about selling it himself. If I remember, we gave him a pretty good price for it."

"Kathryn?" came a deep voice from behind her.

CHAPTER 39

K ate looked up to find Mike Strickland standing behind her. "Oh, Mike. I didn't expect to see you."

Phil stood and he and Mike stared at each other in silence for several seconds. Kate's stomach did a little somersault when Phil put his hand on the back of her chair as if claiming her as part of his territory.

Mike looked from Phil to Kate. "Sorry, Kathryn. I didn't mean to intrude. I thought you said you were meeting a girlfriend here." There was no trace of his charming smile or genial attitude.

Kate felt her face get warm. "Yes. That's right," she blurted out. "I am meeting a girlfriend. But she's not here yet." *I sound like an idiot.* "This is Phil Warren."

Phil reached over the table to shake hands. "I'm a friend of the family," he said coolly.

Mike's expression didn't change. "I'm Mike Strickland. I'm with the Robert Hodges campaign. We're trying to talk Kathryn into volunteering with us."

"You'd be lucky to get her on your team," Phil said and asked the waitress for another wine glass.

"Certainly. I'll bring one right out."

Mike held up his hand, palm out. "No. Don't bring another glass. I'm only staying for a second."

The waitress shifted her eyes between Mike and Phil and shrugged. "Seems to be a pattern," she said under her breath.

As the waitress walked away, Cece breezed in and plopped down in the one remaining chair at the table, her blue eyes sparkling with delight at the scene in front of her. "Well, this is a surprise. I didn't know we were having a group meeting," she said cheerfully. "Did anybody bring a deck of cards?"

Kate felt the tension give way immediately. "Cece Goldman, this is Phil Warren. Phil is . . . a friend of the family." *And don't you dare say anything you shouldn't.*

"Nice to meet you, Phil." The actress was in perfect form. No one could have guessed she'd heard the name before.

"And this is Mike Strickland. He works for Representative Robert Hodges. Hodges is running for governor."

Still no trace of recognition on Cece's face or in her voice. "Good to meet you, Mike."

You really are one amazing actress, thought Kate.

Phil signaled and the waitress reappeared. "I'm guessing you want another wine glass," she said. She turned to Cece. "Are you staying?"

"Yes, of course. And I'm definitely thirsty."

As the waitress turned to go, Mike said, "You can bring a glass for me, too. I think I'll stay for a minute after all."

The waitress rolled her eyes, grabbed four glasses from a nearby stand and returned. "I brought a couple of extras. Just in case anybody else wanders by."

Kathryn tried not to chuckle. *All this and a snarky waitress too. What more could I ask for?*

"Sorry I was late." Cece took off her jacket and draped it over the back of her chair. "The auditions took longer than I thought."

"Auditions?" asked Mike.

"Yes, I'm trying out for a part in a play that's being performed by the local theater company. It's a satire called *Bellevue Revealed*."

The waitress ricocheted back to the table and up to Cece. "I know that play. My sister-in-law is doing the costumes!" She gazed in adoration. "Are you a professional actress?"

"Yes, I am."

"Ooooh. That is so exciting. I want to be an actress someday. Can I have your autograph?"

Cece laughed. "Sure."

"I have a better idea," Mike said. "I'll take a picture of the two of you. When Cece becomes famous, you'll have the photo as proof that you met her." Mike took out his phone and snapped a shot. "Give me your phone number and I'll text it to you," he said as he handed her a campaign button. "And don't forget to vote for Robert Hodges."

After the waitress left the table, Mike raised his wine glass. "Every vote counts." Then he turned his attention to Cece. "They tell me actors make the best politicians. Maybe you should consider working with us on the campaign. Get in on the ground floor of a run for political office."

"No thanks. I have no interest in politics. I prefer to do my acting on the stage. No offense."

"No offense taken. Besides, when you see what a great time Kathryn is having, you'll probably change your mind. If you do, call me." He handed her a card.

Cece looked it over and put it in her purse. "If I decide to volunteer, you'll be the first to know."

Mike checked his watch. "I'd like to stay and talk to you all some more, but I'm already late for dinner with some of our supporters. I better go before they have time to re-think their pledges." He put his hand on the back of Kate's chair, apparently making his own claim, and flashed his smile. "I'll call you tomorrow, Kathryn." He stood and took a last swallow of wine. "Good meeting you, Cece." Almost as an afterthought, he added, "You too, Phil."

As Mike walked away, Cece reached for a menu from the center of the table. "Let's eat. I'm starved! Phil, please join us for dinner. I want to hear all about you and how you know Kathryn."

Kate silently thanked her sister for her exuberance. She had known Cece for less than a week, but she already understood her. *She's trying to make this less awkward for me.*

The three ate dinner and talked about Aristotle, computer science, and acting.

"Do you think you got the part you auditioned for?" Kate asked Cece.

"I thought it went well, but you never know exactly what the director is looking for. It's always a mystery."

"Speaking of mysteries," Phil said to Kate, "did you figure out anything about the note we found on your car?"

Kate put down a forkful of salad. "I did, actually. You see, my father was a great one for puzzles. He often would give me a series of complicated clues to find a birthday present or something like that. Apparently, he had set up another one of these puzzle trails and intended for me to happen onto it around my birthday. The note you found on the car was the first clue. Cece is helping me figure out the rest of the puzzle. The last thing we discovered was this." Kate reached into her purse and took out the pink ribbon with the white writing on the back.

"Find a key unlike all the other keys." Phil pondered the sentence for a minute. "What does it mean?"

"I have no idea. We couldn't find any keys in my house that seemed to fit that description. The only other thing we could come up with was that it was more of a philosophical thing. You know: the key to success, the key to happiness. Maybe Aristotle has a quote that we could use."

"Nothing I can think of." Phil took the last bite of his dinner and checked his watch. "I'd better be going. I've got a class tonight." He went inside the restaurant to take care of his bill. "Ladies," he said on his return, "it's been a pleasure having dinner with you." He addressed both of them but looked only at Kate. Then he left.

"Well, that certainly was interesting," said Cece. "Watching Phil and Mike glare at each other was a lot like a National Geographic wildlife special on mountain goats. I thought they were going to butt heads any second." She laughed. "You had two handsome guys ready to come to blows over you."

"Oh, I don't know about that. Mike seemed pretty interested in you."

"Mike is the smooth type, isn't he? But I don't trust politicians. Most of them are just being nice to get your vote." She lapped up the last spoonful of soup. "But Phil was different. He's not at all like you described him. You said he didn't like you, but I was watching him the whole time. He couldn't take his eyes off you."

"He's certainly changed, but I don't know why. Maybe he's more relaxed because we're not at his shop."

"I don't know what the reason was, but the way he was looking at you made me feel dizzy, and you were acting a little differently yourself. I could almost see the sparks flying between the two of you."

"Sparks? I have no idea what you're talking about, Cece."

"Yeah, right." Cece took a swallow of wine. "Just don't get burned by all those lightning bolts flying around."

Kate signaled the waitress and asked for their check.

"Mr. Warren has taken care of the bill."

"See, I told you." Cece exclaimed as she shrugged back into her jacket. "This is getting very interesting."

Kate laughed and shook her head. "Hey, do you want to get together tomorrow?"

"The theater company is having call-backs, so I may not be available. I'll phone you in the afternoon."

"Great. Talk to you then."

On her drive home, Kate tried to force herself to concentrate on the new clue she and Cece had uncovered, but her mind kept returning to Phil. He was so considerate, so friendly. And she realized she was looking at him differently—not as a handsome man, but as an interesting person, someone she enjoyed being with.

I was completely wrong about him. He really is a decent guy. But why is he all of a sudden showing an interest in me? What changed?

CHAPTER 40

Tuesday

Spring in Bellevue. The time when runners go out to train. The elongated winter had finally settled down. Air that a week ago was frigid was now merely crisp, and the raw wind had resolved into a lively breeze. Athletes who had spent the winter indoors on their kinestatic treadmills were back on the trails, their pale winter complexions glistening with sweat as they were cheered along by the voices of a few early robins.

Kate arrived back at Campbell Park on Tuesday morning intent on hard work. *Hard work. The key to success is hard work.* She shook her head. *I need to stop thinking about this for a while and just let my mind relax. Something will come to me sooner or later.*

She set her GPS and warmed up at the park bench where she had first met Cece. "Just a short and easy three-mile jog today, Barkley. Let's go."

She smiled and nodded at the runners and walkers they passed. Nikes, Asics, and New Balances all pounded by in every imaginable color. Kate looked down at her own gray Sauconys and wondered what they said about her.

Bright people, bright colors. Like Bellevue. *It even means "beautiful view,"* thought Kate. But was it really so beautiful? Or was it just another facade, layered over a core of unhappy marriages, political egos, and attempted murder? Maybe even real murder.

She finished her run back at the park bench. While she was stretching, her phone rang.

"Hi. It's Phil."

"Oh, hi."

"Where are you? I hear birds singing."

"I'm at Campbell Park. I'm training for a marathon, so I'm usually out here on the trails several times a week." She put one foot on the bench and leaned over to stretch her hamstring muscle.

"I didn't know you were a runner."

"Well, this is the first time I've trained for a marathon. It's pretty challenging."

"I bet it is. Hey, I just wanted you to know that I had a great time with you and Cece yesterday."

Kate switched legs on the bench. "So did we. And thank you for the dinner."

"My pleasure. Did you get any further figuring out the message on the ribbon?"

"No. But I'm sure something will turn up. By the way, how was your class?"

"It was good. We talked about the Parthenon, considered to be the epitome of architectural beauty. I thought about what you said about computer science being like architecture, and I wondered what computer system you'd compare the Parthenon to."

"Interesting question," Kate said with a chuckle. "I'm not sure computer science has caught up to Greek architecture yet."

When Phil spoke again, his voice was lower and husky sounding. "Actually, Kathryn, I was wondering if you would do me a favor."

Kate took her foot off the bench and sat down. "Sure, if I can." *What possible favor can I do for him?*

"I told my sister about you, and she wants to meet you. If you're free tonight, I thought we could have dinner at my mom's house. Maybe you could give Molly some advice about job prospects, grad school, that kind of thing."

"I'd love to meet your sister."

"Great. I'll pick you up at seven."

Dinner with Phil and his mother and sister. Am I his date or his friend or his customer?

Kate hung up and walked back to her car. When she got within five feet, she noticed a piece of paper that had been slipped under the windshield wiper on the driver's side. She didn't have to take it off the car. She could read the big, bold letters from where she stood.

"YOU COULD BE NEXT!"

* * *

Tommy Abrahams had just finished straightening his office when the police arrived. He saw the plain-clothes detectives on the security video when they appeared at the door. He buzzed them in and walked to the lobby. *Thank goodness Gavin left early so he won't know about this.*

There were two of them, one short, heavyset, middle-aged. The other tall, thin, and young. The older one seemed to be in charge. "Thanks for meeting with us, Mr. Abrahams. I'm Detective Carlioni." He gestured to the other man. "This is Detective MacMillan."

MacMillan took a small tape recorder out of his pocket and put in on Tommy's desk. "You don't mind if we record our conversation, do you, Mr. Abrahams?"

Nobody had ever called Tommy "Mr. Abrahams" before, and he tried to look sober and mature as he took a seat behind his desk. "You can record if you want to, but I already told the policeman who called earlier that I don't know Clark Bellingham very well."

"But you live in the same apartment building, correct?" Carlioni pulled a slip of paper out of his pocket. "The Blue Post Apartments?"

"Yes."

"That's a pretty small complex, Mr. Abrahams. Only sixteen units total. You must know most of the people there."

"I work a lot. I don't have time to do much socializing."

"But you do know Bellingham."

Tommy shrugged. "We were in a few classes together at the university. I know him well enough to say hello but not much more than that."

"I understand you were at the rally on Saturday."

"Yes, sir. I set up the AV equipment."

"Did you witness the shooting?"

"No. I was behind the stage when it happened. I stick around just in case there are problems with the microphones."

"When was the last time you saw Bellingham?"

Tommy pulled at his ear, trying to remember. "Must have been a week or so ago when I was unchaining my bike to go to work. He came out of the apartment building with another guy."

"Did you speak to him or hear what they were talking about?" Carlioni asked.

"They were pretty deep in conversation. I don't think they even noticed me. But now that you mention it, I do remember something. As they passed by me, I heard Clark say something about a girl."

"A girl? Do you know what girl?"

"I just caught a few words. He said he was going to see Marilyn, or some name like that. That's all I heard."

"Thank you, Mr. Abrahams. You've been very helpful." Detective MacMillan turned off the recorder. "Please don't leave town. We may want to talk to you again."

"No problem. I don't have plans to go anywhere." Tommy felt his chest swell with pride as he walked the two men out of the office. He had done his civic duty. He was helping law enforcement officers bring a dangerous criminal to justice. "I hope you find him soon."

"Don't worry. He can't hide forever. We'll get him."

* * *

"YOU COULD BE NEXT!"

Kate's breath caught in her throat as she stared at the paper. She blinked hard and took a step back. *Get a hold on yourself.* When she looked around to see if anyone was close by, she noticed the other cars in the parking lot had papers on their windshields, too. *What the heck?*

She pulled the paper out from under the wiper blade and flipped it over. There was an advertisement on the back:

You could be the next winner of a trip to the Caribbean!
Register for the Campbell Park 5K and you will be automatically entered in the drawing for two tickets to the Bahamas.
Register now!

Kate leaned against her car and laughed uneasily. "I sure hope they catch Clark Bellingham soon, Barkley, or I'm going to be a nervous wreck."

CHAPTER 41

K ate was folding towels she had just taken out of the dryer when Cece called at lunchtime.

"Hi. How's everything going? Did you figure anything out yet?"

"No, nothing. I'm trying to forget about it for a while. Something is bound to occur to one of us."

"I hope so. It was all I could think of last night. I'm still at the theater, and I'll be here for the next couple of hours. Do you want to get together later today? Maybe we can have dinner again."

She put another towel on top of the stack. "I can't tonight, Cece. Phil has asked me to dinner at his mother's house."

"AHA!" Cece shouted into the phone. "I told you he was interested in you. And he's taking you to meet his mother already. This is moving fast."

"Not at all. He just wants me to meet his sister. She's home from college and studying in the same field that I'm in. That's all. He asked me to give her some advice. You know, the kind of thing a good friend would do."

"Yeah. Just keep on thinking that. What are you going to wear?"

Kate picked up a washcloth from the laundry basket and laid it in her lap. "I hadn't even thought about that. What would you suggest?"

"I guess between the two of us, I have more expertise in outfits," Cece said.

"Yeah, but I don't want to go in disguise." They both laughed.

"Okay, but I can come over this afternoon and help you pick something out if you like."

"I'd love that. Thank you. I'm so used to working at home and running, that all I wear are old blue jeans and running stuff. I need help."

"Great. This is right up my alley. What time is he picking you up?"

"Seven o'clock."

"I'll be over around four, and we'll get you ready for the big show."

"I think you're more excited about this than I am," chuckled Kate as she folded the last towel.

* * *

Cece was precisely on time when she rang the doorbell and Kate let her in.

"No disguise?" Kate teased her sister.

"Not today," Cece said as she stepped into the living room. "This is serious business."

"So, what's the appropriate thing to wear to a dinner where I'm not even sure I'm his date. I think I'm just a friend that he's inviting over to give some advice to his sister. Sort of like helping someone with their homework."

"Trust me, it's a date. You should wear something that's not too dressy but not too casual. Somewhere between an evening gown and blue jeans."

"Well, that narrows the field," Kate said playfully.

"Do you have anything black? Black is always safe."

"Sure." Kate signaled for Cece to follow her. "Come on back to my closet."

The two girls went into the master bedroom closet. Cece was impressed as she slid hangers from side to side, examining Kate's wardrobe. "You have some really beautiful clothes."

"Any nice clothes I have are the result of my mother's good taste. She was the only one in the family with a sense of fashion."

Cece picked out a pair of black slacks that had a slight flair at the hem. "Very nice. Just a hint of formality." Then she pulled out a printed tan and beige silk top with a matching jacket. "This is perfect. Not too fancy. Not too casual. His mother will think you're very sophisticated, but in a nice way."

Kate shook her head. "I sure am glad you're here. I'm not good at this."

Cece found a pair of earrings and a simple gold necklace in the jewelry box. A black clutch and black dress shoes completed the ensemble.

Kate tried on the entire outfit to Cece's obvious approval. "You look gorgeous. But don't wear your hair in a ponytail. Let it hang loose. And call me tomorrow, first thing. I want to know everything."

After Cece left, Kate reflected how much she reminded her of her mother. The way she bit her lower lip as she held up clothes on the hanger to examine them was so much like Leah. And she made it fun, just like Mom used to.

She flipped on the TV to catch the local news. Clark Bellingham was still at large. *It's been three days since the shooting. Why can't they find him?*

CHAPTER 42

Kate was ready by six-thirty. Barkley followed her back to her bedroom and watched while she checked her reflection in the full-length mirror several times.

"What do you think, Barkley? Do I look okay?"

Barkley wagged his tail vigorously.

She patted the little dog's head. "Thanks, buddy. I needed that vote of confidence."

It had been a long time since she'd been on a date. Most of her socializing was in groups, and she rarely paired off with one guy. She'd had a couple of semi-serious relationships over the years, but lately she was content with her life as a single woman. She felt nervous and hoped it wouldn't show.

The doorbell rang at exactly seven o'clock.

Phil was wearing a white dress shirt with an open collar, a blue blazer, and gray slacks. He stepped into the living room. "You look beautiful," he said. "I've never seen you dressed up before."

"This isn't what I usually wear to take my car to the shop. Do you think this outfit is okay? Will your mother approve?"

"I approve," he said with that same wry smile.

Barkley wandered into the room and stood looking up at Phil, politely examining this new human acquaintance. Phil reached down to pat the little dog's head, and Barkley wagged his appreciation.

"Nice dog. What kind is he?"

"He's a border collie. Very smart and very polite. They're sheep herding dogs, but since there aren't any sheep around here, he goes running with me and rounds up a few ducks now and then."

"What's his name?"

"Barkley." The little dog trotted over to Kate at the sound of his name.

"He's awfully short to be named after a basketball player, isn't he?"

Kate chuckled. "He isn't named after Charles Barkley. We called him that because he was such a tiny pup he could hardly bark. Come on in and have a seat. I'll just let Barkley out and get my coat."

When Kate returned, Phil was standing next to the dining room table looking at the flowers. And the note.

"Nice flowers," he said. He pointed to the note. "Is that the same Mike I met yesterday?"

"Yes. Same one." *Time to change the subject.* "I bought a bottle of chardonnay for your mother. Do you think she'll like it?"

"I'm sure she will. Tell me, do you always do everything perfectly?" he asked as he helped her on with her coat.

"Actually, never. But thank you for the compliment."

I hope I don't trip over my own two feet and ruin his impression of me. As they left, Kate stepped very carefully over the threshold.

They arrived at a two-story, colonial-style brick house with a large porch leading to the front doors. Phil parked in the circular driveway in front.

"This is beautiful," said Kate. "You must love living here."

"I don't live here," he said. "I have an apartment in town. This is just for my mother and sister."

Phil took Kathryn's hand, led her into the foyer and called out, "We're here."

CHAPTER 43

A tall woman with a regal bearing appeared from the large dining room to the right of the front hall. She had dark hair, blue eyes, and a melancholy expression. She walked straight to Kathryn and held out her hand.

"Kathryn, I'm Angie Warren. I'm so glad that you could make it to dinner tonight. Phil has been telling us about you, and Molly is very excited to meet you."

"Thank you for inviting me." Kate offered the bottle of wine to Angie. After a few pleasantries, Angie escorted them to the den at the back of the house.

The room was large and comfortable. There was a brown leather couch at one end and a grand piano in the opposite corner, facing out into the room. The lighting was supplied by a few floor lamps, and it gave the room a dark, romantic look.

Angie motioned Kate to have a seat on the couch, and Phil sat beside her. A minute later, a young woman bounded into the room.

Her brown hair was clipped short, and she wore blue jeans and a pink T-shirt. Kate recognized her as the girl she had seen Phil hug at the auto shop.

Molly Warren quickly covered the room and introduced herself to Kate. She hugged her older brother and asked why he hadn't brought Kathryn to meet her sooner. Before Phil could answer, Molly flopped down next to Kate and began to question her on her experience in computer science.

Angie excused herself to check on the cook, and Phil got up to put on some music. Kate immediately took to the younger woman, and they spent much of the time prior to dinner in conversation.

Angie reappeared and led them all into the dining room. A contemporary redwood china cabinet stood against the end wall. The wrought iron chandelier above the table lent an aura of substance and strength to the room. Phil and his mother sat at the ends of the long table, with Kate and Molly on opposite sides. The cook served them a cold cucumber soup, then a delicious chicken casserole.

Most of the dinner conversation revolved around college courses and professional opportunities. Phil kept the discussion light by teasing his young sister about her childish boyfriends and her silly girlfriends.

As apple pie and coffee was served, Angie asked, "Do you like music, Kathryn?"

"I do, but I'm afraid I don't know much about popular music. My parents listened to classical music and that's what I know most about. But I also like music by the Beatles and some early rock 'n roll."

Molly spooned a glob of whipped cream onto her slice of pie. "You like classical music? Who are your favorite composers?"

"I would say Mozart is first. I also like Bach quite a bit."

Phil held his coffee cup between his hands. "Molly also studies music at school. As a matter of fact, in addition to her major in computer science, she has a minor in music. She's quite an accomplished pianist."

"Very impressive," said Kate. "And who are your favorite composers?"

Molly gulped down a forkful of apple pie. "Schubert is my most favorite. I play some of his impromptus. And I like Chopin too. Do you play?"

"I have a piano at home and I play a little, but not very well. I'm afraid I don't have a natural talent for it."

"Molly," Angie said, "why don't you play for us after dinner? It's been quite a while since I've heard you."

"Yes, please do." Kate looked forward to a piano recital from the young college student.

"All righty, but I'm not in good practice right now." She rolled her eyes. "Too many exams lately."

The group moved into the den for the performance. Molly asked Kate to sit next to her as she played. During the next half hour, Molly went through a Mozart sonata and several pieces by Chopin while Kate turned the sheet music pages.

As they came to the end of the short recital, Kate glanced at Phil and saw him gazing steadily at her. He made her feel like there was no one else in the room, just the two of them, and she felt a little light-headed at the thought. She was brought out of her trance when Molly played the final chord of the Chopin etude.

After the three spectators had voiced their approval, Phil suggested it was getting late and he had to work the next day, so they prepared to leave. Molly made Kathryn promise to keep in touch. The two young women exchanged contact information and embraced each other. Kate thanked her hostess for the evening, and she and Phil left.

As they settled into Phil's car, Kate reflected on how enjoyable this evening had been, even though she had been so taken with Molly and so aware of Angie that she had hardly spoken to Phil all evening. She leaned her head back against the head rest and turned to him. "That was lovely," she said.

"You were lovely, and I'm glad you and Molly had a chance to meet."

While they drove, Kate said, "Your sister is very talented. I was impressed with her playing."

"She is very talented. She can come across as silly sometimes, but she's actually very focused. She works hard at everything she does."

As he parked the car in front of Kate's house, she asked, "Are you as musically talented as your sister?"

Phil chuckled. "No, not at all. They tried to get me to play the piano when I was a little boy, but I had no interest in it. I remember once when my mother made me practice I was sitting in front of the piano thinking, 'There are too many keys. And they all look alike!'"

Kate's mouth dropped open as she drew in a sharp breath. "A key unlike all the other keys."

"Are you thinking what I'm thinking?" asked Phil.

"I bet I am. The clue must have to do with the piano. Would you like to come in and let's take a look at it?"

"You bet I would."

CHAPTER 44

Inside the house, they made a beeline to the studio piano standing in front of the window in the living room. Kate opened the lid of the piano, and they both looked in. Nothing but the strings and mechanism. They examined the keyboard and its cover. Still nothing. While Kate opened the top of the piano bench, Phil slid under the instrument to check the underside of the keyboard.

"Aha!" he said.

Kate got down on the floor next to Phil. He pointed to a key taped to the underside of the keyboard. Lying on their backs on the floor, they turned toward each other and smiled.

Phil carefully peeled back the tape and removed the key. After they crawled out from under the piano, he handed the key to Kate and stood behind her, his hands on her shoulders. She tried to concentrate on the discovery and ignore the warmth of his hands.

"Another step closer to the truth," she said.

"What do you mean?" Phil asked as she turned around to face him. They were standing as close as they had that day in the auto shop, but this time she did not retreat.

"I told you about how my father loved puzzles," she explained. "When I was a little girl, he used to say, 'Puzzles are our friends. Solve a puzzle and you're one step closer to ultimate truth. Solve a puzzle and you're one step closer to God.' So, we've made another step in solving this one."

"Okay then, let's solve this puzzle. Do you recognize this key?" he asked.

"No. But it looks like there's a number imprinted on it." She moved to an end table and held the key under the light of the lamp. "One hundred and twelve—that's the number."

"Can I see it?" Phil took the key and examined it. "It's small. Maybe it fits a filing cabinet or a desk."

For the next half-hour they tried the key in various locks in Kate's house. She had taken possession of her father's desk, but it wasn't locked to begin with, and the key didn't fit anyway. Nor did it fit any of the filing cabinets in her house. She had a small lock box, but the key was too large for that.

After they exhausted all the possibilities they could think of, she suggested they take a break. "Something will turn up. It always does." She laid the key on the coffee table. "Would you like a glass of port or a cup of coffee or something?" *Please say yes.*

"A glass of port sounds good."

While Kate got the glasses and bottle from the kitchen, Phil found the CD player and put on a '50s rock 'n' roll album. He browsed through the bookcases that lined the living room walls. "You have a pretty impressive library here," he called out to her.

"A lot of the books belonged to my father," she said as she brought in the wine and glasses. "I can't bring myself to get rid of them."

Phil picked up a book that was lying on a small table next to a bust of Aristotle. "Have you been reading this?"

"Yes. After our conversation, I decided to do a little research on Aristotle."

"Good choice," he said as Kate handed him a glass of port. They sipped wine and talked about life in Bellevue.

"Show me pictures of you growing up," he said.

"I'll show you some pictures, but only if you promise not to laugh." She pulled down a couple of photo albums from the bookshelves. The two of them sat together on the couch with the photo albums open on the coffee table in front of them.

Phil flipped through each page, obviously enjoying the embarrassment some of the early pictures were causing Kate. He stopped on one picture that showed a kindergartener Kate standing in between her two parents, holding a large certificate in her hands. She had a big smile on her face, exhibiting a lack of a couple of baby teeth. "Kindergarten graduation day," she said.

"Can I take a picture of that one?" Phil asked.

"You don't mean it."

"Yes, I do." He pulled out his phone and took a photo of the picture. Then he sat back, stretched his arms out on the back of the couch, and looked pleased with himself.

They sipped wine and talked until one o'clock in the morning. When the Everly Brothers came on singing "Let It Be Me," Phil stood and held out his hand. "Dance with me?"

She took his hand, and he led her to an open space in the living room. Phil held her in an unassuming waltz position as they began a slow two-step to music that spoke of the blessing of newly discovered love. She felt his right hand press gently into the small of her back. As he pulled her closer, she did not resist. He gazed steadily into her face.

Phil put both of his hands on her waist and drew her still closer while the soft rhythms of the song enveloped them.

They had almost stopped moving now, just barely swaying to the music. As his mouth gently caressed her face and neck, Kate put her arms around him as much to steady herself as for the desire to embrace him. His arms were tight around her waist.

Let it be me.

While the Everly Brothers offered their vocal encouragement, Aristotle stood by, observing the swaying couple, as if contemplating the inward significance of two souls longing to be one. Phil kissed her gently, then harder, then deeply and passionately. He did not release her until the music stopped.

When the song ended, Phil drew back and looked intently into her eyes. He held her close with one hand while he gently brushed her hair back from the side of her face with the other.

Kate was aware of her heart beating hard against her chest. Or was that his heart? She moved her fingers over his crisp, white shirt and felt his muscles tense under her touch.

Finally, he took her hand and led her to the front door. "Can I call you tomorrow?"

Kate managed an unsteady yes. He leaned down, kissed her again, and whispered, "Good night, beautiful."

After he left, Kate dropped onto the couch, shaky and flushed. She stretched out fully and sighed, reliving the last few moments and savoring the taste of him in her mouth. After several minutes, she stood and sauntered down the hall to her bedroom, humming with the music.

All I have to do is dream.

She slept soundly that night, and she did dream. She forgot to turn off the CD player, and the Everly Brothers stayed up and sang all through the night. And she completely forgot about the little key that was lying on the coffee table in her living room.

CHAPTER 45

Wednesday

"What happened? Tell me everything." Cece's eager voice came across the phone at eight o'clock Wednesday morning.

"We had a wonderful dinner, and I enjoyed being with his family." Kate wasn't sure what to say about the previous night, but she answered all her sister's detailed questions about Phil's mother, the dinner, and what Molly was like. Suddenly she remembered the key they had discovered, and she told Cece how they figured out it was under the piano.

"I see," Cece said, with more than a hint of sarcasm. "We've been talking about Phil and his family for thirty minutes, and you just now remember you discovered the next clue in the puzzle that's been consuming your life for the last week? Sounds like you've changed your priorities, sister."

Kate giggled. "I guess you could say that. Can you come over this morning? I'll show you what we found."

"You make the coffee. I'll be there in half an hour. I can't wait."

When Cece arrived, she stood in the doorway staring at her sister. "Kathryn, you look positively radiant. What happened last night?"

"I have no idea what you're talking about," Kate said as she led her sister back to the kitchen for breakfast.

"Don't give me that. You're glowing." Cece stood with her hands on her hips, looking skeptically at Kate. "Something happened beyond just dinner with the family. You don't have to tell me if you don't want to, but there's no use denying it."

Kate poured the coffee. "Okay. Phil brought me home and we found the key under the piano. We talked for a while and he asked me to dance. Then he kissed me goodnight. Have a seat and drink your coffee."

Cece plunked down in her chair, looking incredulous. "I take it that's the abridged version. We can talk about this more, but you may have to wear a veil over your face so the glow doesn't blind me."

Kate laughed and reached over to hold her sister's hand. "Oh Cece. My head is just spinning. Last night was so wonderful. But I need to think about it a while before I can talk about it."

"Okay, sister. But whenever you're ready, I want to hear everything."

She showed Cece the key. "This is what we found, but we couldn't find any lock in the house that it fits. I'm not sure where to go from here."

"How about a sports locker?" Cece asked. "Did your father belong to a gym?"

"Yes, he did. That's a good suggestion. I'll go over there this afternoon. Want to come with me?"

"Oh, I got so excited about your date that I forgot to tell you. The director called last night. I got a part in the play! It's a small part, but I'm really thrilled. I have to go for a costume fitting this afternoon, though, so I can't go with you. Call me and let me know if the key works at the gym."

"Cece, I'm so happy for you. What part did you get?"

Cece grinned mysteriously. "I'm not going to tell you. You'll have to come see the performance."

"I can't wait."

After Cece left, Kate sat at her kitchen table staring at the little key when the phone rang.

"Hi." It was Phil.

"Hi," she responded softly.

"I was just sitting here thinking about you."

"Really? What were you thinking?"

"I don't think I can tell you that."

She imagined the wry smile on his face, and a sensation of warmth spread over her.

Phil's voice took on that low, husky quality. "Will you have dinner with me tomorrow night? No parents or siblings, just you and me."

"I'd like that."

"How about The Embers?"

"Okay. I love it there."

"Good. I'll pick you up at seven."

Kate hung up and sat back in her chair with a big smile on her face. She returned to her closet to pick out something to wear. *I'd better call Cece later to see if she can help me with this.*

CHAPTER 46

Commissioner Blake's rubber-soled shoes squeaked on the tile floor as he strode down the hall toward the detectives' offices. Police headquarters was eerily quiet, given the frenzy over the shooting. The feds were out trying to whistle up leads, and much of the Bellevue police force was scouring areas that Bellingham was known to have frequented. But the trail was cold. Glacial. Maybe Carlioni and MacMillan had something.

Blake pushed open the office door at the end of the hall and addressed the detectives. "Any good news for me today, boys?"

Carlioni was behind his desk, slumped over a map. He looked up. "Sorry, boss. We got nothin'. This guy Bellingham just disappeared into thin air. Even the feds can't find him."

Blake moved farther into the room and leaned against an old file cabinet. "Have you checked with his family? His friends?"

"His parents say they haven't been on speaking terms with him for a long time. The friends we found didn't know anything, and the folks at the university have no idea where he is."

"Somebody must know where he went. Did he have a girlfriend?"

"Nope. This guy is a real loner."

Detective MacMillan looked up from his laptop. "That one guy mentioned a girl,"

"What guy?" Blake asked.

MacMillan picked up a spiral notebook and flipped through the pages. "Tommy Abrahams. He works over at ArcTron Labs. He said he overheard Bellingham say he was going to see somebody named Marilyn, right Carli?"

"Yeah. But we checked around and we couldn't find anybody named Marilyn who has a connection to Bellingham." Carlioni waved his hand in the air. "Abrahams must have got it wrong."

Blake frowned. "So, all we've got to go on is somebody named Marilyn, and that's probably wrong." He took a roll of Life Savers out of his pocket and popped one in his mouth. "All right, boys. Keep at it. We need to find him. And we need to find him soon. I'm tired of the mayor calling me every fifteen minutes."

As he started for the door, he noticed a calendar hanging lopsided on the wall. He straightened it and stared at the picture of Mount St. Helens on the front cover. He took a couple of steps back and rubbed his chin with his hand. "Hey, guys. Come over here and take a look at this." He pointed to the calendar. "What do you see?"

Carlioni and MacMillan joined him in front of the bulletin board.

Carlioni spoke first. "An old calendar that's way outta date. That's what I see."

"What about you, Mac. What do you see?"

"A picture of a volcano," MacMillan said.

Blake took the calendar off the wall. "You know what I see? I see a woman's name." He pointed to the caption under the picture. "Helen."

Carlioni squinted at the commissioner. "What are you gettin' at, boss?"

Blake put the calendar back on the wall. "What if Marilyn isn't a girl? What if it's a place? When Bellingham said he was going to see Marilyn, maybe he meant he was going to a place called Marilyn. A town or a mountain or something. What d'ya think?"

Carlioni cackled, "I think that's why you're the chief and we're just a couple of dumb detectives." He smacked the back of his partner's head as he headed for his desk. "Mackie, get on that computer of yours and start looking for places named Marilyn. I'll check the map and see what I can find."

MacMillan was already typing. "It could be something that sounds like Marilyn," he said. "Maybe Maryland or Marlin or something."

"Good point," Blake said as he walked toward the door. "Report back to me in an hour with what you find."

* * *

Kate took the key to the health club her father had belonged to. She asked the man behind the desk if it might fit one of their lockers. "We don't use keyed locks," he said. "All our lockers have built-in combination locks."

When she got back to her car, she called Cece and told her about this latest dead-end. "By the way, how was your costume fitting?"

"Great. I can't wait for you to see it."

"I'm excited for you, and I'm really looking forward to your play." As she started the car, she added, "Hey, could you come over tomorrow? Phil asked me to dinner, and I'd like you to help me pick out another outfit."

"I'd love that!"

There was something else Kate wanted to talk to Cece about too. But that would have to wait till she saw her sister face-to-face.

* * *

At five o'clock Wednesday afternoon, Kate received a call from Mr. Kaplan. The police had found Clark Bellingham in a remote campground called Merlin Park deep in the foothills. They had taken him into custody.

"Thanks for telling me, Mr. Kaplan. It's good to know I'm no longer in danger."

"This doesn't necessarily mean you're out of danger," he replied. "There's a lot that we still don't know, and you have to be alert until this case is closed."

"Sure. I'll be careful," she said. But she was already thinking ahead to her date with Phil.

CHAPTER 47

Phil was sitting with his hands behind his head and feet propped up on his desk when Ben cruised in.

"Evenin', sport," Ben said as he took his usual seat.

"Good evening, Ben." Phil took his feet down off the desk and faced his friend. "How's everything going?"

Ben scowled. "Well, I'm just havin' a peachy keen time. Jerry tore up the transmission on a Camry this afternoon, and we're going to have to put in a new one. A heck of an expensive mistake, and it doesn't do us any good in the customer satisfaction department either. You've got to talk to Jerry about his carelessness. He's a smart guy, but he gets in too much of a hurry. That's the second big mistake he's made in the last month."

"No problem. I'll handle it."

"And while you're at it, the guys who are supposed to reset all the systems on the used cars are letting some of them go out with Bluetooth information and GPS stuff still set up with the previous owner's info. Kyle Langley called to say he had to reset everything himself on that Prius he bought. We need to make sure this stuff doesn't happen again."

"Okay." Phil grinned and nodded.

Ben stopped short and looked carefully at his friend. "Are you listening to me?"

"Sure. I'm listening."

Ben raised one eyebrow and tilted his head to the side. "You look a little distracted, sport. Anything goin' on you want to tell me about?"

"No. Not really."

Ben nodded slowly. "Well, that's interestin'. I've only seen that dazed expression on a couple of men in my life. One was a guy on TV who had just won the lottery for a hundred million dollars. The other had something to do with a girl."

CHAPTER 48

Thursday

"You don't think it's too formal for a dinner date?" Kate asked as she eyed the floor-length black dress Cece was holding up.

"It's perfect!" Cece said. "Very elegant. Modestly sexy."

Kate took the hanger from her sister. "You're sure?"

"I'm positive," Cece said as she searched through Kate's jewelry box. "Ah." She picked out a pearl necklace and long, swingy earrings. "Showy in a nice way," she said.

"I had no idea there was such an art to getting dressed. And I never realized so many of my clothes are black. It's kind of morbid, don't you think?"

"I think you'll look fabulous, whatever color you wear. But wear your hair up. It'll make you look more sophisticated and show off your neck. He'll be smitten. Actually, he's already smitten. You'll just seal the deal. Now, put it on and let me see."

Kate slipped into the black dress and twirled around for her sister. "Do you think the slit in the back is too high? It's above my knees."

"Too high?" Cece responded. "Some dresses have a slit all the way up to the hip." She shook her head. "You don't get out much, do you?"

They both laughed. "Obviously not. Not only do I not know what to wear, I really don't understand anything about men. I'm at a pretty big disadvantage here. I need your advice on everything."

"Advice is right up my alley, sister. What do you want to know?"

Kate changed back into a T-shirt and blue jeans, and she and Cece moved into the living room. Kate brought in cups of tea and a plate of cookies.

"I just don't know what to think about Phil. For the last five years, I would take my car to his repair shop, and I had the feeling there was something about me that just rubbed him the wrong way. Like he was trying to get away from me as fast as he could.

"Now, all of a sudden, he's completely changed. He's friendly and attentive, even romantic. I'm confused about all of this. He's only a few years older than I am, but he's so much more mature and worldly. I know he's a serious man because of how he's taken care of his family, but I also know he could have any woman he wants." She put her teacup on the table and pointed to the window. "And there are plenty of beautiful women out there who'd like to take advantage of that. I can't believe he's more attracted to me than to them." She grimaced. "Is it possible I'm just another girl he's decided to seduce?"

Cece nibbled at her cookie. "No way. From what you've told me about him, he's really decent. I can't imagine him running around with a lot of girlfriends."

Kate leaned forward with her elbows on her knees. "This is going to sound strange, but when Phil and I spent Tuesday evening together, I felt like I had known him all my life—as if we were two halves of the same whole. Everything we talked about, everything we did, just seemed to fit. I've never felt like this about a man. But it all happened so fast, I'm not sure if I'm imagining it. I feel completely out of my depth." She shook her head. "Am I getting ready to get hurt?"

Cece set her teacup on the table. "Kathryn, listen to yourself. You're saying this guy is Mr. Wonderful, but you're afraid of getting hurt. First of all, he'd be a lunatic to think you're not perfect when anybody can see that you are. But suppose something happens and it doesn't work out. That's not the end of the world. That's just life."

Cece hesitated as if weighing whether she should say what was on her mind. "Can I be totally honest with you?"

"Of course."

"Your mother once told my mom something I think you should know. She talked about how you were brilliant, kind, talented. You know, all the things we told you before. But she said there was one thing about you that concerned her."

"Really?" Kate sat forward. "What was it?"

"She said everything came easily to you. You got good grades without having to try very hard. You had a nice group of friends. You did volunteer work in the community. Your life was without any real obstacles, always very comfortable for you. But she said you stayed inside a kind of insular environment because it was safe, and that worried her."

"An insular environment? What does that mean?"

"It means not willing to take a risk. She told Mom about a pottery-making course you took one summer, but you dropped out because you weren't good at it."

"I was terrible." Kate giggled, remembering it. "You should have seen my vases; they all leaned to one side." She made a slanting gesture with her hands. "And those were the good ones. There was no need to continue to do something that I clearly had no talent for."

Cece took a sip of tea. "That was exactly her point. She was afraid you wouldn't work for something that might result in a failure. She worried that you'd never risk a serious relationship because it might mean having to move beyond your comfort zone, and you weren't willing to do that."

Kate sat back on the couch and hugged her knees. "It's true I've always been afraid of failure. But to take a chance at messing up the most important relationship of my life is beyond scary."

Cece put her cup down and looked intently at her sister. "I've been told that the relationship between a man and a woman is the highest expression of the human experience. But it isn't like one of your math problems, Kathryn. There's no formula for getting it right. It's unique for each couple and you have to work at it even if you're not sure of yourself.

"You don't know where this thing with Phil is going. Yeah, you might get hurt. Maybe he's deceiving you. Could be he's not the man you think he is or that you want him to be. Listen, all of that might be true, but you can't run away. You have to take a chance.

"Don't you suppose Phil took a chance that you might reject him the other night? What if he'd been afraid to make a move? The two of you might still be exchanging insignificant how-de-dos at the repair shop and miss the opportunity of a lifetime."

Cece pursed her lips together and leaned forward. "Look, I'm not sure what love is, but if you think you may have found the one guy for you, you can't take a chance and let it go."

Kate put her feet back on the floor and leaned over to stroke Barkley's fur as she reflected on what she just heard. "I never thought of myself as running away, but you may be right." She embraced Cece and said, "Thank you, sister. I've never had a talk like this with anyone before. I'm so glad you came into my life."

Cece gave the remainder of her cookie to Barkley and returned to her usual, lighthearted banter. "I can't wait to hear how it goes tonight. Call me tomorrow. First thing!"

CHAPTER 49

Kate had bought the long, black dress a year ago for an evening party at her software firm, but she had gotten sick at the last minute and couldn't attend. As she examined her reflection in the full-length mirror, she was glad this was the first time she had worn it. For some reason, that made it special.

Phil arrived wearing a suit and tie and carrying a bouquet of flowers. As he stepped into the house, he looked her up and down. "Wow," he said. "You look gorgeous. Where'd you get that dress?"

"What? This old thing?" she said coyly, surprised at how comfortable and confident she felt.

"Mmmm. Here, I brought you some flowers. I know you're into ribbons, so I even got one of those for you." He held out the flowers to her. The pink ribbon tied around the bouquet of roses had a message written in white ink. It said, "Hello, Beautiful."

"They're lovely. Thank you." She reached for the blooms.

Phil pulled them back and grinned. "It's gonna cost you."

"You can't charge for a gift," she said and took the flowers. "I'll find a vase and put them in some water." As she walked down the long hall toward the kitchen, she heard Phil utter a prolonged "Mmmm" again.

He followed her into the kitchen. "I have an idea. Let's cancel our dinner reservations. I'm sure we can cook up something here."

Kate threw him a look over her shoulder that said "you are a naughty boy." She took a vase down from the shelf and stood at the kitchen sink, running water in it for the flowers. Phil moved in close behind her at the sink and gently stroked and nuzzled her neck while she tried to take the flowers out of the plastic wrap they were in. Finally, she abandoned the flowers and turned to him. They stood spellbound in the moment, his arms encircling her waist and hers around his neck. He drew her in and kissed her intensely.

Barkley had been following the two around and now he stared at them, as if wondering what this strange new game was that his owner was playing. He woofed to let them know he should be included.

Kate looked down at the little collie. "I think he's jealous."

Phil reached down and ruffled Barkley's ears. "Sorry, old pal," he said. "You'd better get used to it. You've got competition."

CHAPTER 50

The maître d' at The Embers showed them to a quiet corner table. Kate thought the restaurant had never seemed so beautiful. She and Phil stayed for three hours, laughing, eating, and sharing their life experiences.

As they were finishing beef tenderloin dinners, Phil said, "I sure am glad we've gotten to know each other these last few days. You know, I was mistaken about you. You aren't anything like I thought when I met you five years ago."

"You mean the first time I brought my car into your shop?" She took a sip of wine.

"Yeah. I got the impression you thought my greasy situation was beneath you. Like you were too good to be associated with a mere mechanic."

"Nothing could be further from the truth. Where did you get that idea?"

He reached over the table and took her hand in his. "Don't you remember the conversation we had that day?"

"Sort of. I don't remember it exactly."

"I remember it. When I saw you come in, I walked over and introduced myself to you. I was trying to be real polite." He squeezed her hand and grinned. "Then you just shut me down."

Kate grinned back at him, remembering that day. "I did not shut you down."

Phil continued. "Yes, you did. You called me Mr. Warren. Like I was some middle-aged old codger with a beer belly and a pontoon boat in the backyard. Like you were just humoring me with your presence."

Kate giggled. "I didn't think you'd want to talk to me. You were important and serious, and I was just a silly school girl with an old car. I was shy and nervous."

"You didn't look nervous to me," Phil teased, and he squeezed her hand again. "You looked all high and mighty, and you blurted out something about how your father told you to bring your car in. You handed me the key and ran away so fast, I thought you must be training for the hundred-meter dash."

Kate blushed and laughed. "I was afraid of you."

"Not only that, but you gave Ben Mullins enough material that he could razz me about you every time you brought your car back into the shop. I'm not sure I can ever forgive you for that."

Kate tilted her head to the side and leaned toward him. "So, what made you change your mind about me?"

"Somebody told me something that made me realize I had it all wrong."

"Who was it? What did they say?"

"I'll tell you sometime, but not now."

The waitress came to the table with coffee, and they sat back so she could fill their cups.

Kate took a sip and said earnestly, "I was so intimidated by you. My father used to tell me how smart and wonderful you were, and I figured you wouldn't want to spend any time talking to a nerdy girl."

"Your dad said that about me?"

"Yes. He was very impressed with the way you ran the business. He mentioned it to us more than once."

Phil poured cream in his coffee. "Your father was my favorite customer. He'd always drop by my office when he came in to the shop, and we'd spend a few minutes talking. He was really a great guy, the kind of person I'd like to be. I wish he was still around; I'd like to get to know him better. You know, he did something once that impressed me so much it changed my life."

"Really?"

Phil sat back and propped his elbows on the arms of his chair. "About five or six months ago, your dad brought his car into the shop to have the engine overhauled. You know how your father kept a car until it was dilapidated."

"Yes," she remembered her father's penchant for saving money. "This car is perfectly good," he'd say when asked why he would maintain such a mechanical atrocity. He was a generous man with friends and family, but he was penurious with his own belongings.

"We had to do a lot of work on that car, and the final bill came to a couple thousand dollars. Your dad came by to pick it up, and he paid the bill and left. An hour or so later, he called our bookkeeper to say there was a mistake on the bill. She assumed we must have overcharged him since that's the only reason anyone ever calls to report a mistake. But he told her she'd added up the total incorrectly and we had undercharged him by several hundred dollars.

"She was so flustered she put him on hold and called me. We looked at the bill and he was right. She had neglected to include one of the charges that was almost five hundred dollars. I told your dad to forget it. It was our mistake. But he wasn't having any of that. He said he'd come back and pay the correct amount, and he did just that. He didn't wait for another time, and he didn't accept the offer to forget the oversight. He just drove back and made out another check."

"That was Dad, all right. He used to say we should never let money get in the way of doing the right thing."

"When he came back in, I met him and took him on a tour of the shop. I introduced him to some of the guys and invited him into my office. We spent a couple of hours talking to each other that afternoon. We covered some pretty interesting topics. That was the last time I saw him."

Kate was grateful for this new memory to cherish. "He was a wonderful man. Thank you for telling me that story."

Phil took another swallow of coffee and asked her to tell him about how she and Cece met.

Kate explained that her mother had been a friend of the Goldmans. "Mom had emailed Cece's mother on the day of the car accident. The Goldmans thought there might have been some kind of foul play involved, and they contacted me."

"Foul play?" Phil frowned and leaned forward in his chair. "Really?"

"It's probably nothing, but there are some questions about the accident. The police even think Clark Bellingham may have been involved."

"You mean the guy the police were looking for after the shooting at the political rally?"

"Yes. They found out he had been in one of my father's engineering classes and Dad had given him a failing grade. They think he may have held a grudge against my father. Personally, I find that hard to believe, but I'm glad they found him and can question him. I just want to know the truth about what happened. I was hoping the string of clues my dad left might help us solve the mystery. I'm still trying to figure out what the key means."

"Did you make any progress today?"

"No. Cece thought it might belong to the sports complex where my father was a member, but they told me they don't have keyed lockers there, so we're back to square one."

"Well, at least you've eliminated some of the possibilities. I still have your parents' automobiles on my lot. Maybe your dad put something in one of the cars that the key would fit."

"I hadn't thought of that."

"Why don't you come over in the morning, and we'll take a look." He hooked his fingers into hers. "That'll give me an excuse to see you tomorrow."

"Can I bring Cece?"

"Of course."

On the ride home, they were quiet. After Phil parked the car in front of her house, he reached over and gently laid his hand on her shoulder.

She looked into his eyes. *If there was just one feeling I could hold on to for the rest of my life, this would be it,* thought Kate.

They walked to the front porch hand in hand. Phil opened the door for her and stepped aside.

"Aren't you coming in?" she asked.

"No."

She tilted her head to one side quizzically.

He took both of her hands in his. "Kathryn, I want to be honest with you. You have totally dazzled me. I can't get you out of my mind. I think about you constantly. I want to call you just to hear your voice. I want you so much it scares me, and I'm afraid if I come in, I won't be able to control myself. I don't know what this is, but I don't want to take a chance on messing it up."

For her part, Kate was grateful for his chivalry, but disappointed at the same time; perhaps more disappointed than grateful. "All right, then. Good night, Phil." She reached up, kissed him on the cheek, and turned to go inside.

But he held her and pulled her back to him. "Not just yet," he grinned.

CHAPTER 51

Friday

Kate's phone rang at eight o'clock Friday morning.

"I want to know everything," Cece said.

Kate answered all of her sister's eager questions about the previous evening, and she asked if Cece would like to go to the repair shop to try the little key on the Frasiers' cars.

"Absolutely, I want to go. I have to go to the theater later, so I'll drive separately. I'll meet you there at ten."

At nine o'clock, Mr. Kaplan called. The police had released Clark Bellingham. "They questioned him, but he denies the shooting, and they don't have any hard evidence, so they had no choice but to let him go. Please be careful and alert."

Kate frowned, but even the news about Bellingham could not dull her happiness. "Thanks, Mr. Kaplan. I'll be careful."

Kate and Cece arrived at Phil's shop and found him in his office. Instead of his usual blue cotton shirt and denim jeans, he was wearing a golf shirt and casual slacks.

Kate noticed a framed photo on his desk. It was her kindergarten graduation picture. Lying on the desk in front of it was a copy of Jane Austen's *Pride and Prejudice*.

As Phil escorted the girls to the lot, Kate thought she saw Ben Mullins elbow one of the other mechanics and nod toward them.

204 • KAY DIBIANCA

"The cars are over here," Phil said and led them across the lot. "Are you going to be all right with this?" he asked Kate.

She nodded. "I'll be okay."

They checked each car to see if there was something the key would fit, but to no avail. "Not even close," he said. "Sorry I brought you all the way out here for nothing."

Cece was standing behind Kate and nudged her as if to say, "Yeah, I'll bet he's sorry."

Phil asked to see the key again, and Kate handed it to him. "It must have something to do with the number," he said. "One hundred and twelve."

"What are you thinking?" she asked.

"Could it be an address?"

Kate twirled her ponytail around her fingers. "I can't think of any familiar address with those numbers."

"Maybe it's an area code."

Cece checked her phone, but 112 wasn't a valid area code.

Phil had another idea. "Do you suppose it could be the key to a safety deposit box?"

Kate considered it for a minute. "But which bank? There are a lot of banks in town. We can't just walk into each one and ask if our key fits one of their boxes. They won't let us. Dad wouldn't have set up an impossible problem. He would have included information about which bank it was."

The three got quiet again.

One hundred and twelve. One-one-two. Kate snapped her fingers. "Wait a minute. I have an idea. Maybe it is a safety deposit box key, and the bank's address is embedded in the clue."

"How could that be?" Phil asked.

"My father loved number series. One of his favorites was the Fibonacci series."

"The Fibo-whatsit series?" asked Cece.

"Fibonacci. It's a number series that starts with 'one-one-two.' Each number is added to the previous number in order to calculate the next number in the series. So, the first few numbers are one-one-two-three-five-eight, and so on. If he was using the Fibonacci series, and if it is a safety deposit box, the next several numbers in the series may be important. Does that seem too far-fetched?"

"Nothing is too far-fetched for this puzzle," said Cece as she leaned back against the car.

"So, you think the numbers three-five or three-five-eight may have something to do with it?" asked Phil.

"It sounds crazy, but it's the kind of thing my father would do. Maybe there's a bank in town with three-five or three-five-eight in the address. Or the phone number."

"Let's go take a look." Phil was already walking toward the building.

Back in Phil's office, he pulled up a list of banks in the area on his computer and spotted it. "First Bellevue Bank, 358 Appleton Square. That's a newly developed area of town. I'll bet it's a new branch. Can you wait until this afternoon to go to the bank? I have a customer coming over this morning who's having trouble with a car we sold her. She wants to see me personally, so I need to be here."

"I'm too anxious to wait." Kate was already punching the address into her phone. "We'll drive over there now. I'll call and let you know what we find. Good luck with your customer."

Cece trotted out to the lot behind Kate. "I'll follow you," she said.

* * *

Becky Fielding flounced into the lobby of Warren's Auto Repair Shop wearing a red polka-dot dress, red patent leather stiletto heels and very red lipstick. Her platinum blonde hair sprang up and down as she clacked her way across the tile floor to the reception desk.

"Is Phil here?" she demanded. "I have an appointment."

"Yes, ma'am," replied the receptionist. "I'll page him."

Phil walked into the hall to meet her. "Hi, Becky. I hear you're having some problems with that BMW you bought from us. Come on in my office and tell me about it." He checked his watch. She was thirty minutes late for their appointment.

He knew this visit was motivated by more than a couple of automobile issues. Becky had been making it clear for a long time that she was available and would like Phil to take advantage of that fact. He avoided her when he could, but both her parents and two of her brothers were good customers, so he had to give her his time when she made an appointment, as she had today.

He escorted her into his office and left the door open. Becky took a seat across the desk from him. "I hardly know where to start, Phil," she pouted as she smoothed the skirt of her dress. "There are so many things wrong. The windshield wipers don't clean well, I have trouble getting the gas cap off, the accelerator pedal sticks, and I just don't understand how to set up all the stuff on the console. I haven't even been able to get my phone to work with Bluetooth yet. Can you help me?" She batted mascara-laden eyelashes.

"Sure. Let's have a look." Phil checked his watch again. Almost noon. *Maybe I can get this over with soon so I can call Kathryn and see what she's found.*

CHAPTER 52

K ate and Cece met in the parking lot of the bank and entered together. Kate asked to see one of the bank's officers, and they were shown into the office of Mr. Adam Johnson, Vice President.

Kate explained that her parents had died several months earlier, and she had just come into possession of a key that appeared to be for a safety deposit box. She took the key out of her purse and handed it to him. "It has the number one hundred and twelve on it. Can you tell me if it's one of yours?"

"I'm so sorry to hear about your parents, Miss Frasier. Let me see if it's in our system." Mr. Johnson entered some information into his computer. "Yes, here it is. That safety deposit box was bought by Dr. Frasier less than six months ago."

Mr. Johnson read more of the information on his computer screen. "It says here he left instructions that his daughter, Kathryn, should have access. If you have some identification, I can allow you to open the box."

After verifying her ID, Mr. Johnson retrieved the partner key from his safe, and the two women followed him into the vault. He took the key from Kate and inserted it into the lock of box 112; then he inserted his key into the second lock. Both keys clicked to the right effortlessly, and he extracted the safety deposit box from its cubbyhole. He handed the box to Kate and showed the two women into an adjacent room where they could examine the contents. "Take as long as you need," he said as he left.

Kate set the box on the small table and stared at it for a few seconds. "Aren't you going to open it?" asked Cece. "I'm dying to see what's in that box before I have to go for my costume fitting."

"I'm a little afraid. I'm not sure what we're going to find." Kate took a deep breath and lifted the lid.

The large safety deposit box was completely empty with the exception of a nine-by-twelve-inch manila envelope. The handwriting on the back of the envelope said "For our Special K."

"What does that mean?" asked Cece.

"My dad used to call me his Special K, so I guess it means this is for me." She picked up the brown envelope, unsecured the clasp and opened the flap. She drew out a set of papers and laid them on the table. "This looks like a patent application."

Kate scanned through the document and saw that it was a specification for some kind of electronic device. A large Post-it note was attached to the last sheet. It had her father's handwriting. "Congratulations! You are one step closer to ultimate truth."

Kate explained this sentence to Cece who had not heard about Dr. Frasier's puzzle adage.

The note continued: "This patent application should be approved soon. I expect that it will be worth a great deal of money and, should it be approved, the proceeds will be your birthday gift. I know you will use the money wisely."

Kate sat down in one of the chairs, overcome with the emotion of the moment. Her father had always told her to spend her money wisely. Here was one last compassionate bit of advice from him. *So like him.* She brushed away a tear.

"Funny," she said. "We found what we were looking for. We solved my dad's puzzle, but I don't feel fulfilled. I feel . . . heartbroken."

"Heartbroken?" said Cece. "Your father gave you a wonderful gift. How could you feel bad?"

"The whole time we were trying to figure this out, I thought we'd find out more about my parents' deaths, something that would make sense out of it all. I was wrong to get my hopes up like that. I should have known Dad was just leaving clues to guide me to a birthday present."

Cece put her hand on her sister's shoulder. "I'm sorry. I realize how disappointed you must be. But even if you didn't learn more about the accident, you should follow up on this. Shouldn't you have been notified if your father received a patent for his invention?"

"Maybe the patent wasn't granted. It happens all the time. They probably just didn't want to bother me if it had been denied." Kate put the documentation back in the envelope.

Cece put her arm around Kate's shoulder. "Listen, I know you're sad, but you should get in touch with your dad's company. Maybe the approval process is still going on. At least you can find out about the work he was doing in his last months. It would honor your father to get the details on his invention."

Cece's compassion and good sense won the day. Kate clipped the envelope shut and patted her sister's hand. "You're right. I'll call Gavin Connelly."

While Cece went to find Mr. Johnson to put the safety deposit box back into its place, Kate phoned Gavin and explained that she had found a patent application her father had been working on. "Did you know about it?"

"No. I didn't know your father had applied for a patent recently. Why don't you bring it over to my office so I can take a look at it."

"I know it's Friday afternoon, Gavin, and I'm sure you're looking forward to the weekend. I'd be happy to wait till Monday morning if that works better for you."

"No, no. I'm sure this is important to you. Come on in and let me take a look."

"Thank you so much, Gavin. I can be there in an hour or so."

Cece returned with Mr. Johnson. The three saw the empty safety deposit box replaced in its slot and Kate retained the key. They thanked the bank officer and left the building with the manila envelope firmly in Kate's hands.

Cece looked at her watch. "Oh my gosh. I'm late to pick up my costume. I have to rush. Did you get in touch with Gavin? Are you going over to ArcTron?"

"Yes. I'm going to stop and grab a sandwich first and then go over there. I talked to Gavin, and he offered to look at this today. Do you think you can make it over there after you pick up your costume?"

"I'll try, but it might take a while if they have to do alterations. If I don't catch up with you at ArcTron, I'll call you later. Good luck!"

Kate stopped at a deli for lunch and called Phil.

"Hey. Did you find out anything?" Phil asked.

Kate could hear a woman's voice in the background saying something about windshield wipers.

"I just left the bank. You were right. The key was to a safety deposit box. We found an amazing package that my dad left for me. It's a patent application for an invention of his. I'm on my way over to ArcTron Labs to have Gavin Connelly take a look at it. Give me a call when you finish with your customer."

"Will do. It might take a little longer than I thought, but I'll call you."

CHAPTER 53

Phil spent almost an hour dealing with his finicky customer, covering just about every inch of her car. Becky had him checking the oil, the car fluids, the tire pressure, the windshield wipers, and anything else that would keep him occupied and in her company. Finally, she insisted they go for a short ride to experience the "bumpiness."

Phil was beyond exasperated. "Okay," he said. "But I have another appointment, and I can't be gone more than a few minutes."

"That's fine," she cooed as they got in. She drove.

* * *

Kate left the deli and jogged across the parking lot to her car. Storm clouds had gathered in the sky while she was inside having lunch. She slid into the driver's seat and checked the weather forecast on her phone. *Chance of severe thunderstorms. I hope they hold off until I can finish all of this patent business with Gavin.* She dropped her phone into the cup holder of her car and started over to ArcTron Labs.

Kate parked in the rear parking lot. The only other car there was Gavin Connelly's silver Mercedes. She picked up the manila envelope with the paperwork, exited her car, and walked toward the building.

"Miss Frasier?" said a voice from behind her.

She turned around and saw a man step out from the shadow of a tree. As he walked toward her, she gasped. There was no mistaking that face. It was Clark Bellingham.

Where did he come from? She couldn't get back to her car. He was between her and the vehicle. *Stay calm. Sound like you're in control.* She took a deep breath. "Yes. What do you want?" she said as firmly as she could.

"I need to talk to you." Bellingham looked tense. The left side of his face was twitching.

Kate stiffened. "I can't talk now. I'm meeting friends here."

He moved closer. "The police took me into custody. They thought I shot Representative Hodges." He frowned. "Did you tell them that?"

Kate felt her heart pounding and could hear her own breathing. "Of course not."

He moved closer still. "They asked me if I had anything to do with your father's death."

Why did they ask him that? "I'm sure it's just a mistake. I certainly don't believe you had anything to do with my father's death."

He stopped about ten feet from her. Kate cringed at the sight of his matted hair and grungy clothes and she eased backward.

"Your father failed me in an engineering course, but . . ." He seemed to lose his train of thought and rubbed his forehead. She took another step back.

Should I run? The only way out of this parking lot is past him. If I keep backing up, he'll have me pinned against the building. I can't go inside. He might follow me in and we'll be alone in the hallway. What if Gavin isn't there? I need to take a stand here.

Kate pulled herself up as tall as she could. "I have a meeting in this building now. You'll have to leave."

Bellingham took another step toward her with his arm outstretched. "I just need to talk to you for a few minutes."

Kate felt the hair standing up on the back of her neck, and her body tensed all over. *In a few more steps, he'll be within striking distance and I'll have to run.* She took a deep breath, preparing to make her move.

"Kathryn. Is that you?" A voice called from behind her. She looked back and saw Gavin at the door of the building.

She uttered an audible sigh. "Oh, Gavin, thank goodness you're here."

Bellingham took several steps back, turned, and ran out of the parking lot.

Gavin came over to Kate's side. "Who was that?"

"That was Clark Bellingham."

"The suspect from the shooting? That was him?"

"Yes. He must have followed me here. Listen, can we go in the building? I don't feel safe out here."

"Of course." He took her arm and walked her inside.

As they entered the ArcTron offices, they encountered Tommy Abrahams with his laptop slung over his shoulder. "Kathryn," he said. "What's wrong? You don't look well. Are you all right?"

"I'm okay. Clark Bellingham just surprised me in the parking lot. Fortunately, Gavin came out. I think I should call the police." She rummaged through her purse for a minute. "I must have left my phone in the car. Can I borrow one of yours?"

"Tommy," Gavin said, "take Kathryn to the break room and get her a bottle of water. I'll call the police and report it to them."

As Tommy and Kate walked down the hall, their footsteps echoed in the empty building. "It's so quiet here," she said.

"Yeah, everybody leaves early on Friday. Gavin and I are the only ones left in the building. I usually stick around till five o'clock, but Gavin told me I could go on home. I was just about to leave when you came in."

When Tommy and Kate returned to the CEO's office, Gavin was just getting off the phone. "The police said they'll pick Bellingham up immediately for more questioning. That should take care of him. In the meantime, I've remotely locked the outside doors, and the inside door is always locked. You'll be safe here with me. I'll walk you out to your car after we've had a chance to look over the patent paperwork."

"What patent paperwork?" Tommy asked.

Kate explained, "I found a patent application my father was working on. Since Gavin files all the patents for ArcTron, I was hoping he could tell me the status of this one."

"That's really exciting, Kathryn," Tommy said. "Mind if I stick around to hear about it?"

Gavin gave him a critical look. "No need for you to stay, Tommy. I know you were about to head out. I'll let you know if we find anything interesting."

"I'd like Tommy to stay," Kate said. "He worked with my father on several projects, and I'd like to have his opinion."

Gavin gave a tight little nod. "All right. If you insist."

CHAPTER 54

"**B**ecky, I need to get back to the shop now," Phil said firmly. "I have another appointment."

But Becky still had issues. "Just one more thing," she whimpered. "I can't get the GPS to work. I put in the address of my hairdresser, but now I can't find it." She pulled into the parking lot of a small shopping center and looked at him with pleading eyes. "Can you show me?"

He sighed. "If you put in a destination and want to look at it again, all you have to do is hit the 'Previous Destinations' button on the GPS screen." He pressed it and a list of addresses popped up. The top one was Becky's hairdresser. But it was the second entry that caught his attention. Martindale Hotel. Reno, NV. Phil frowned and quietly mouthed the words, "Reno, Nevada."

"Becky, did you put in this entry?" he asked, pointing to the screen.

"No. I only added one address. The one for my hairdresser. I've never been to Reno, but I'd love to go sometime," she squeaked as she reached over and touched his hand that was still pointing to the entry.

Phil quickly opened the passenger door. "Sorry, Becky, but I've got to get back to work right away. Let me drive."

Phil took over and flew back to the shop. He hopped out and ran onto the repair floor looking for Ben Mullins. Ben was working on an old Ford Bronco. "Ben, do you remember the car we sold to Becky Fielding? Whose was it?"

Ben looked past him out to the lot where Becky had been left standing next to her BMW. "That midnight blue BMW? That was Gavin Connelly's car. Remember, he sold it to us and bought that fancy new Mercedes? Why? Something wrong?"

"That's what I thought. I just noticed a GPS entry for Reno, Nevada. But Gavin told me he'd never been there before last weekend. I have a feeling something's not right. Listen, Ben, I've got to get over to ArcTron Labs right away."

Ben frowned at the urgency in his friend's voice. "You need me to come with you, son?" Ben had only referred to Phil as "son" twice before: once when Phil's father died and again when he volunteered to work for Phil at a reduced salary until the young man could get his business up and running.

"No, just take over here." Phil was punching Kate's number into his phone as he ran toward his car. No answer.

alm down. The danger is over. Kate took a long drink of water as she and Tommy took their seats in Gavin's office. "Thanks for giving me a minute to collect myself. I feel better now."

"That's great, Kathryn," Gavin said. "Now tell me about this patent application you found."

She explained that she had come across the paperwork her father had left her as a birthday gift. "Dad told me you always negotiated the patent sales, so I'm sure you must be aware of this." She held the envelope out to Gavin.

He took the folder to his desk, removed the document from the pouch, and leafed through the pages. When he got to the last page, he laid the paperwork to one side and sat motionless for a minute, frowning and chewing on his lower lip.

Why is he looking so serious? Was the patent denied? She looked over at Tommy. He looked worried.

Gavin walked around his desk to the empty chair next to Kate, sat down, and took her hands in his. "Kathryn," his voice registered concern. "I don't know how to tell you this." He sighed and dropped his head down. Out of the corner of her eye, she could see Tommy squirming in his seat.

Gavin looked up. "Your father had been assisting me with a project I'd been working on for several years. It was a secret project, one that even the other employees didn't know about. A few months ago, I had a breakthrough and filed for the patent."

Why is he telling me this? I want to hear about Dad's patent, not his.

He paused and shook his head sadly. "I'm really sorry, Kathryn, but it looks like your father copied my data and tried to file it as his own idea. I doubt it was ever entered."

Kate pulled her hands out of Gavin's. "You're saying my father was going to copy your work and claim it as his own? That he was going to cheat you?"

Gavin nodded. "I'm sorry, Kathryn, but that appears to be the case."

"That's impossible!" Kate jumped up. "My father would never do something like that."

Tommy scrambled to his feet. "Dr. Frasier wouldn't have done what you're accusing him of," he said to Gavin. "There must be some other explanation."

Gavin stood and faced Tommy directly with an expression of simmering anger on his face. "What other explanation is there? This is an exact copy of the patent application I filed months ago. What else could it be other than professional theft?"

Tommy's face reddened.

Gavin put his hand on Tommy's shoulder in a gesture of conciliation and added in a softer tone, "Look, Tommy, this matter doesn't really concern you. It's been a long week. Why don't you go on home and get some rest. Kathryn and I can talk this out together."

Gavin walked Tommy to the office door and patted him on the back. "I'll see you on Monday."

Tommy looked back at Kate sympathetically and left.

She heard the outer door open and close, and she was left alone in the office with Gavin.

* * *

Phil kept hitting "redial" on his phone as he raced toward ArcTron Labs, but Kate didn't answer. *Kathryn, where are you? Why don't you pick up?*

He rounded the corner at Center Street and glanced at his watch. He was still minutes away from ArcTron.

CHAPTER 56

K ate was shocked and hurt that Tommy had abandoned her so quickly just because Gavin had challenged him. *Is he so afraid of losing his job that he turns his back on his friend?*

"Look, Gavin. I don't know what's going on, but I know my father would never do what you're accusing him of. There's something fishy here, and I'm going to get to the bottom of it."

She marched over to Gavin's desk and snatched up the patent document. As she turned back, she saw Gavin lock the office door with a key from the inside.

Gavin's face registered a haughty disdain. "Sorry, Kathryn, but I can't let you do that."

Kate stopped next to the chair she had been sitting in. "What are you talking about? What do you mean?"

"We both know your father was an agent for the CIA, and he was trying to entrap me."

Kate stared in disbelief. "That's crazy!"

"Don't you dare say that to me!" As he spit the words out, his face contorted into a menacing furor, and he shook his fist wildly at her. "Don't ever say that to me!"

Kate stood motionless, gaping at the deranged figure in front of her, aware that she was alone in the building with him. And she had no idea what he was going to do.

She held onto the back of the chair to steady herself. *I've got to get out of here.*

"Look, Gavin. I know you're upset." She tried to sound calm and self-assured as she put the envelope on the chair. "Maybe it would be better if we talk about this next week. I'll just go on home now, and I'll call you on Monday."

"Do you really think I'd fall for that?" Gavin snickered. "I suspected all along that you were one of the conspirators in your father's little espionage circle. Now I see I was right. You're going to pay for what you and your father tried to do to me."

Kate suddenly became hyperconscious that everything in the office was black, white and gray. The furniture, the bookshelves, Gavin's suit. As if life itself had been bleached out of the room. She shuddered when she thought how her black warm-ups and gray running shoes fit so well into this awful picture.

Should I scream? It's likely no one would hear me in this insulated building, and even if they did, he could do a lot of damage before anyone came—if anyone came. I don't think I can overpower him. Besides, he locked the door from the inside. There's no way out.

She fought back the tears that were forming. "Gavin, I really don't know anything about this. I'm your friend. Please let me go home."

"You're not going anywhere." Gavin started walking slowly toward her. Kate took a step back and looked around to see if there was something she could use as a weapon. But this sleek office had nothing to offer.

ever give up. As Gavin edged closer, Kate planted her feet and prepared to fight. The only sound in the room was her own breathing. And Gavin's.

But then she heard something else. A scrape and a click. A key turning in the lock.

Tommy Abrahams opened the door of Gavin's office and stepped in. His shirt was soaked through with sweat.

Kate's jaw dropped open. "Tommy!"

Gavin shouted at him. "I told you to go home. How dare you disobey my order!"

Tommy didn't answer, but quickly moved across the room to Kate's side. He put his hand on her arm, and she could smell the pungent odor of his sweat. "I wasn't going to leave you here alone," he said softly. "I just had to check something."

Tommy faced Gavin and spoke with a boldness Kate had never seen in him before. "I knew Dr. Frasier wouldn't steal your work. So, it must have been the other way around. I remembered there were a lot of emails going back and forth between you and him during the months before he died. I suspect those emails will show that you were getting the information from Dr. Frasier on his invention."

"There are no emails, you fool," Gavin scoffed. "Frasier's laptop was destroyed in his accident, and all the backup emails were lost in the server crash due to your incompetence. Now get out of my office."

"That's where you're wrong. About a year ago, I opened a trial account with a third-party vendor for backup. You were away on business, but I thought it would be a smart thing to do. When you got back, you went into a tizzy because one of the accountants had ordered some software without your approval. You fired him, and I was afraid you might fire me if you found out about my moving ahead on my own.

"The emails between you and Dr. Frasier are on that backup server." Perhaps for the first time in his life, Tommy Abrahams smirked. "We'll see who's lying."

Gavin's eyes squinted almost shut as he reflected on what he had just heard. "I won't tolerate this kind of insolence in my company," he hissed. "You know the rules. You can't make any decisions without my approval. You're fired. Leave your badge and key on my desk and get out."

"That's what I thought you'd say. If I leave now, you might be able to figure out how to remove those emails from the other server. That's why I called the police. They're on their way. I've unlocked all the doors so they can get in. I'll make sure they know exactly where to look for the truth."

He had barely completed the sentence when the lobby door opened, and a dark, heavyset policewoman with a severe expression on her face came in. She was wearing a gun on her hip and, striding quickly, she covered the outer lobby area and walked directly into the CEO's office and up to Gavin. Gavin's face went white with panic, and in one maddened movement, he grabbed her sidearm and shoved her violently. She hit her head on the credenza and collapsed in a heap behind the couch.

Gavin's eyes were large and wild as he pointed the gun at Kate and snarled, "Little Miss Smarty-Pants. Well, you outsmarted yourself this time." He leveled the gun and aimed. Tommy quickly stepped in front of her.

Gavin shot twice. Tommy doubled over, grabbing his midsection, and tumbled onto the floor. Gavin ran out of his office and escaped through the lobby door.

CHAPTER 58

Phil's car screeched to a halt in front of the ArcTron building. As he sprinted to the door, two loud bangs split the air. *Are those gunshots? Kathryn!*

He rushed into the front entrance and spotted Gavin making his escape out the back.

Phil raced through the lobby to Gavin's office. A policewoman lay slumped on the floor behind the couch. Kate was leaning over the body of a man lying in the middle of the office.

When she saw Phil, Kate jumped up and ran to him. "Phil, call an ambulance," she said. "Tommy's been shot!"

He grabbed her by the shoulders. "Are you all right? Are you hurt?" His eyes were willing her to be unharmed.

"I'm okay. But call 9-1-1. We need an ambulance for Tommy."

As Phil reached into his pocket for his phone, the policewoman stirred and pulled herself to her feet. "What's going on?"

* * *

Kate and Phil stared in disbelief at the policewoman whose black wig was partially askew, revealing curly, blonde hair. "Cece, is that you?" Kate shrieked.

Her sister gingerly touched the side of her head where it had hit the credenza. "I think so."

Kate put her arm around Cece's waist to steady her. "What are you doing here? And why are you wearing a gun?"

Cece wobbled slightly and looked bewildered. "What gun? That's not a real gun. It's just a prop. This is my costume for the play. What's going on? Why did Gavin push me?"

Phil turned Tommy onto his back. "There're no gunshot wounds. He must have fainted."

Kate kneeled beside him and gently shook his shoulder. "Tommy, wake up. You're okay. They were just blanks."

Tommy's eyelids fluttered and then his eyes popped open. "Blanks?" he said, and then grinned sheepishly as they helped him to his feet.

Gunshots resounded from outside. They ran to the window and saw Gavin standing beside his car firing at police officers. Kate screamed at the police. "Don't shoot. It isn't a real gun." But the window couldn't be opened, and the building was too well insulated for people outside to hear.

It only took one shot, and Gavin went down. By the time they got outside, the police were standing over the still body of Gavin Connelly. The fake gun was lying beside him.

* * *

Policemen and detectives arrived and spent several hours questioning the four young people. Kate called Reverend and Mrs. Whitefield, and they rushed over to ArcTron Labs. Cece phoned her parents, and they hurried over as well.

Kate explained how Tommy had stepped in front of her to protect her from Gavin, and Reverend Whitefield offered prayers of thanksgiving for the safety of them all and especially for Tommy's extraordinary courage.

Dear Tommy. All these years she thought she should look out for him. But when the ultimate test came, Tommy Abrahams was there for her. "You were willing to take a bullet for me." Kate held the hand of her childhood friend while he shuffled his feet and blushed at his sudden prominence.

Cece approached and stood in front of her sister with tears in her eyes. "You did it. You found the final piece of the puzzle."

The final piece of the puzzle. It was all beginning to make sense.

The two young women embraced each other and wept.

CHAPTER 59

Wednesday

K ate sat on her couch with the old photo album open on
the coffee table in front of her. She turned the pages
slowly, her fingers softly touching each picture in turn,
as the memories settled around her.

Cece hadn't been exactly right. Kate still didn't have all the
pieces to the puzzle. There were empty spaces in the story, but
she and Phil would drive to Mr. Kaplan's office today to learn the
details Kaplan had pieced together. Then it would be finished.

Her phone buzzed with a text from Phil. ON MY WAY. TEN
MINUTES.

Kate dropped her phone into her purse and noticed the in-
vitation to the inauguration Mike had left for her. Five days had
passed since the awful events at ArcTron Labs, and Mike hadn't
called. Maybe he was traveling and hadn't heard about it. More
likely, he didn't want to get involved. Wasn't sure how it might
impact the campaign.

How sad. Everything filtered through voter polls.

Phil was a different story. They had spent every day together since the shooting. He was her rock, and she wasn't running
away. She was falling.

When she returned the album to its place on the bookshelf
behind the couch, it knocked over a framed picture. She picked

up the photo of her with her parents, taken when she was a teenager on their last camping trip together. A sudden storm had inundated the campground, leaving the bedraggled family standing in mud up to their ankles in front of a partially collapsed tent. A fellow camper had snapped the picture of the three of them, soaked pajamas clinging to their shivering bodies and smiles of delight on their faces.

Kate sighed and put the picture back in its place. Then she grabbed a jacket and walked out to meet Phil.

When they arrived at Kaplan's office, the others were already there. In addition to Kaplan, the group included the Whitefields, the Goldmans, Cece, Tommy, and Commissioner Blake. After warm greetings all around, the participants positioned themselves around the room so they could all see and hear as the story unfolded.

Kaplan buzzed his assistant. "Carolyn, we don't want to be disturbed until the meeting is over." Then he moved in front of his desk to address the group. "I'm glad you could make it here today, and I'm happy to see you all looking well." His eyes scanned the group and landed on Kate. "We have quite a story to tell, so let's get started."

Kathryn felt her stomach tighten. The final piece of the puzzle was about to be put in place.

Kaplan gestured toward Blake. "Commissioner Blake and his team have been hard at work searching out the details of Gavin's past, and they've put together a complete chronology of events for us. Let's begin with the episode that took place in Gavin's office last Friday. Commissioner, why don't you start us off?"

Blake propped himself on the arm of an empty wingback chair. "First of all," he said, "I want to commend Cece on her Oscar-worthy performance. Young lady, I doubt you ever imagined that your impersonation of a police officer would turn out to be the most significant role of your life."

"No, of course not. I just thought it would be funny to go to ArcTron in costume and see how long it would take my friends to recognize me." Her expression became somber. "I keep wondering what would have happened if I hadn't done that. Maybe things would have turned out better."

Blake shook his head. "It probably would have been worse. It was very good fortune you came in when you did, dressed the way you were. Gavin was apparently in such a state of agitation it's hard to know what he might have done. My officers found a loaded gun in his desk, and it's possible he would've used it if you hadn't come in when you did."

Kaplan interjected, "And Tommy's expert administration of the computer systems at ArcTron Labs gave the police all the information they needed to confirm Gavin's guilt. If it hadn't been for that backup server, they might never have been able to prove that Gavin stole Dr. Frasier's patent idea."

Tommy replied, "I was sure there was some funny business about those missing emails, but I couldn't find the root cause of the crash. It finally dawned on me when Gavin accused Dr. Frasier of theft that Gavin himself must have erased the emails on our server and covered his tracks. It was a big shock to him when I told him there was another backup system."

Blake agreed. "It was a big shock all right. Big enough to push him to attempt murder."

"But why would Gavin want to steal Dad's patent?" Kate looked puzzled. "He was a successful man in his own right."

Kaplan walked around his desk and settled into his large executive chair. "Commissioner Blake and his team uncovered some details about Gavin's past that nobody knew. He was a heavy gambler. The police discovered he was in debt up to his eyebrows, and some pretty bad people were telling him to pay up. Or else."

Kate and Tommy both spoke at once. "But he told us he hardly ever gambled."

Kaplan rested his elbows on the desk. "That's a common thing for someone with a gambling addiction to say. It's like an alcoholic who hides his drinking and tells people he only has a glass of wine now and then. It's a facade, designed to mislead people who might have a lower opinion of them if they knew the truth.

"Gavin needed a lot of money, and he needed it fast. When Bill Frasier came to him with an idea for an electronic device that looked sure to be extremely profitable, Gavin convinced him to keep it a secret so he could sell the rights to the patent himself and pocket the money."

"But that meant he had to sell the patent without Bill Frasier knowing about it," said Reverend Whitefield. "Or find a way to get Bill out of the way."

"Unfortunately, he decided on the second option," Commissioner Blake said. "The authorities in Nevada helped us put together a picture of what happened the weekend the Frasiers were in Reno."

"So, Gavin played a part in the automobile accident?" Kate stared grimly ahead. She had hoped that Gavin was only guilty of theft, not murder.

Kaplan looked over the tops of his rimless glasses. "Kathryn, Commissioner Blake and I are going to describe the events in Reno that led to your parents' deaths. Do you want to hear this now, or would you prefer to step out of the room?"

"I want to hear it."

CHAPTER 60

K ate took a deep breath. She held tightly to Phil's hand and silently prayed for strength to hear the story of the disastrous car crash for the last time.

Commissioner Blake cleared his throat. "Our detectives checked the hotels in the immediate vicinity of the one where the Frasiers were staying that weekend, but Gavin Connelly wasn't registered in any of them. However, Phil provided the information that Gavin's old car had the Martindale Hotel in Reno listed as a previous GPS destination. Gavin made one crucial mistake when he paid for dinner at the hotel with his credit card. That confirmed the location of the meeting."

Kate sighed and shook her head. "He told us he'd never been to Reno before. I guess that was just another lie. It's amazing how readily I believed everything he said to me."

Harry Goldman spoke up, "Not surprising at all, Kathryn. You are a trusting person who never had reason to believe you were being lied to. I'm afraid you've received an unfortunate, but probably necessary, lesson about life."

Blake pulled a small device out of his pocket and held it up to the group. "Our colleagues in Nevada provided us with proof of the meeting. This thumb drive contains hotel garage videos that show Gavin escorting the Frasiers to their car in the garage after dinner. He seated Dr. Frasier in the front passenger seat and helped Mrs. Frasier into the back seat. It's possible he may have drugged them. Gavin drove the car out of the garage at approximately seven o'clock."

"Where did they go?" Cece asked.

"There's no way to know exactly what route they took. Gavin may have stopped to buy gasoline in order to ensure that there was plenty of flammable liquid on board. We're in the process of checking surveillance videos from nearby gas stations. It's likely that he drove the car up to a place on that lonely mountain road where there was no guard rail, aimed the car at the edge, put it in drive, and got out. The car simply rolled over the edge and crashed hundreds of feet down the embankment. If the Frasiers had been alert, they certainly could have stopped it. That supports the police theory that they were drugged. A full tank of gas would have guaranteed there would be a terrible fire and death."

Kate dropped her head into her hands and sobbed quietly. She couldn't bear the thought of her parents being helpless in their final moments. She silently prayed that they had been unconscious and hadn't understood what was happening to them.

Phil put his arm around her and pulled her close. Jan Whitefield patted her shoulder.

Commissioner Blake waited until Kate raised her head and wiped her eyes. "Please go on," she said.

He continued. "The hotel garage video revealed that Gavin returned to the garage on foot around nine o'clock. That's consistent with a scenario of his driving to the road departure point, causing the accident, and walking back to the hotel. He didn't reenter the lobby of the hotel, but simply got in his car and left."

"Is that enough evidence to prove he committed murder?" Phil asked.

"No, but I think we all know the truth." Blake sat down in the wingback chair.

Mr. Kaplan picked up the narrative. "Gavin contacted a manufacturing company and finalized negotiations to sell the rights to Dr. Frasier's proposed patent, which he claimed as his own. The rest of the story is clear. He received a huge payment and used it to settle his debts. It was the answer to all his problems. Of course, he wasn't aware that Dr. Frasier had hidden evidence of his patent and intended it to be found by Kathryn on her birthday. From that point on, you all know the story."

Kate dabbed her eyes with a tissue. "If Gavin had just told me the patent was denied, I would have believed him. He'd have been completely in the clear. Why didn't he do that?"

Kaplan theorized that Gavin was so surprised by Kate's bringing the documentation to him that he wasn't able to hatch a rational plan on the spur of the moment.

"He was irrational all right," Kate said. "He started screaming at me and saying crazy things, like my dad was in the CIA and I was one of his spies. It felt like one of those nightmares that don't make any sense but there's no way out. I thought I was done for."

Phil tightened his arm around Kate.

Kaplan pointed to a copy of the patent application lying on his desk. "When you told him you were going to figure out what happened with the patent, his entire world started to crumble. His mind probably couldn't bear the fact that he was caught in his own web, and I'm guessing he just snapped. He had to get rid of you too, and the CIA business was a way for his sick mind to justify it."

"But it all turned back on him," said Harry. "He sowed the wind and reaped the whirlwind."

Kate asked, "So Clark Bellingham wasn't involved in my parents' deaths after all?"

"That's right," Commissioner Blake answered. "Bellingham didn't have anything to do with the shooting at the political rally either. He was just in the wrong place at the wrong time, and everything pointed to him. We learned a few days ago that a drifter from California had been bragging to his friends about having shot Hodges. The local authorities tracked him down, and he confessed to the attempted murder. Bellingham is a free man."

"When Clark approached me in the parking lot of ArcTron, I was scared out of my wits, but he was probably just trying to explain things to me. How sad."

Blake leaned back in his chair. "Bellingham told the police that he went over to the building to see Tommy, but you drove up just as he got there. He wanted to make sure you knew the truth, but when Gavin came out, he got scared and left."

"So now we know the entire story," Reverend Whitefield said.

Kaplan stood, an indication that the meeting was coming to an end. "Truth has a way of revealing itself," he said. "It's like a splinter you get in your finger and it just festers there until it comes out. Then the healing can begin."

Commissioner Blake stood and addressed Kate and Cece. "I'm extremely impressed with the work you ladies did on this case. If you're interested, there might be some potential for the two of you in police work. Just something to think about."

The two girls looked at each other and both broke out laughing. "No way," Kate said. "I don't ever want to be involved in anything like this again."

"I second that," added Cece. "I'm done with detective work, but I'm glad we finally know everything about the accident. In spite of the pain, I think knowing the truth really does set you free." She smiled at Kate. "Now that this is over, we can move on with our lives."

Sylvia stood and put her hand on Cece's shoulder. "But it isn't completely over, is it dear?"

Cece's face reddened.

Sylvia continued. "Dearest, you have to face the truth once more. You have a biological parent whom you must meet. It's time."

Cece frowned at her mother. "I'm not sure I'm ready."

Harry stood and put his hand on Cece's other shoulder. "It's your choice, Cece. We'll support whatever you decide."

Kaplan offered, "If it would make it any easier, Cece, I can set up a meeting with all of you in my office."

Kate realized that her sister was now going to face a crisis of her own. She and Cece exchanged a long look, then Kate nodded her support.

"You're right," Cece said to her parents. "It's time."

Another truth was about to be revealed.

CHAPTER 61

As Phil drove Kate home, she told him about her mother's young affair with Robert Hodges and her recent discovery that Cece was actually her half-sister.

Phil issued a low whistle. "You've been keeping all this inside you? I wish you'd confided in me."

"I should have. I know that now. But things were happening so fast I hardly knew what to do."

"How do you think Hodges will react when he meets his daughter?"

"I have no idea. I met him a couple of weeks ago, and I'm not sure what to think about him, but I'm going to be there when she tells him."

Phil stopped the car in front of Kate's house and turned to her. "Won't that be hard for you? After all, what he did was the source of some very bad things."

"Probably. But I need to be there for my sister."

* * *

John Kaplan took a deep breath and punched the numbers into his cell phone.

"Representative Hodges's phone. This is Elizabeth Howley. May I help you?"

"Hello, Elizabeth. John Kaplan here. I'm calling for Bob. Is he there?"

"Hello, Mr. Kaplan. Yes, Representative Hodges is here, but he's in a meeting right now. Is your call urgent?"

Kaplan knew that being "in a meeting" just meant Hodges wanted to be able to decide whether or not he would take phone calls. "Not urgent, but it's very important that I speak to him."

"All right. May I put you on hold while I see if he can come to the phone?"

"Certainly."

A few seconds later the genial voice of Robert Hodges was on the line. "John! Good of you to call. What can I do for you?"

"Bob, I was wondering if you could drop by my office one day soon. There's a new family in the area I want you to meet."

"I'm always happy to get to know my supporters—or potential supporters," he said with a chuckle. "Who are they, John?"

"Sylvia and Harry Goldman and their daughter Cece. I don't want to be mysterious, but I would like you to meet them in private. Kathryn Frasier will be there, too. They're all available tomorrow."

There was a brief pause on the line before Hodges replied. "Very well. I can drop by tomorrow afternoon at two if that's convenient."

"That's fine. See you then."

Kaplan clicked off his phone and laid it on his desk. "Finally," he said softly.

CHAPTER 62

Thursday

Kate arrived at John Kaplan's office on Thursday afternoon at one-thirty and found Cece and her parents already there. She could feel the tension in the room. Even Mr. Kaplan seemed nervous as he paced the floor, occasionally asking if anyone wanted water or coffee.

She pulled a chair up next to Cece and asked her sister how she was feeling. Cece was uncharacteristically serious, but she was sure this was the time.

Finally, the receptionist buzzed, "Representative Hodges is here to see you."

"Send him in."

Hodges entered the office wearing his right arm in a sling. "Sorry I won't be able to offer my right hand as usual," he said as he extended his left hand to Kaplan. Everyone in the room stood.

Kate fought back against the hostility that was rising up inside her. *Let it go. He's about to get the shock of a lifetime.*

Kaplan began the introductions. "These are the people I want you to meet." First, he pointed out Kathryn.

Hodges nodded to her. "Good to see you again, Kathryn."

She nodded in return.

Kaplan introduced him to Sylvia and Harry Goldman.

Finally, he guided him over to Cece. "This is Cece Goldman."

Hodges and Cece stood in the center of the room, facing each other. His usual confident expression evaporated, and he stared wistfully at her. His voice was barely audible. "Cece Goldman."

Cece took a shaky breath but spoke clearly and decisively. "That's my adopted name. Cecelia Leah Goldman. I was born in 1980. My biological mother was Leah Dawson."

There was complete silence in the room as everyone waited for Hodges to respond. Kate could hear her own heart thudding against her chest and wondered if anyone else could hear it. *What is he going to do?*

Hodges responded quietly, "I know who you are."

Several of the attendees gasped when they heard this last statement. They had expected Bob Hodges to be in shock, but instead, they were. Mr. and Mrs. Goldman and Kate all sank into their chairs. Only Cece, Kaplan, and Hodges remained standing.

Cece's mouth dropped open in surprise. "You know?"

Kaplan stepped up to the side of Hodges. His voice had lost its usual authoritative tone and sounded incredulous. "Bob, are you saying you already knew that Cece Goldman is your daughter?"

Hodges didn't take his eyes off Cece. "I know that Cece was born in March of 1980 to Leah Dawson and is my biological daughter."

Once again, there were murmurs of shock.

Hodges continued, "I'll explain."

"Yes, please do," responded Kaplan. Now he sat down as well, leaving Cece and Bob Hodges facing each other in the center of the room.

Hodges motioned toward Kate. "A couple of weeks ago, Tommy Abrahams brought Kathryn over to campaign headquarters, saying she might want to volunteer. During the introductions, he mentioned that her parents' names were Bill and Leah Frasier. I was startled by the name. I've only known a couple of people named Leah in my life. Of course, there was no reason to believe Leah Frasier was the woman I knew as Leah Dawson, but it made me look at Kathryn very carefully."

He turned to her now. "Kathryn, you don't look much like your mother, but when I heard that name, I thought I saw some of Leah's expression on your face. It made me wonder if it was possible that Leah had given birth to our child secretly, something I had never even considered before. At that moment, I questioned in my own mind if Kathryn could be my daughter."

"Me?" Kate spoke up in surprise.

"Yes. You looked to be about the right age. It got me thinking that, if Leah Dawson was your mother, you could be the child I had asked her to abort. After you left the office that day, I asked Mike Strickland to find out everything he could about you, including your age."

So that's why he asked me to dinner. And why we spent so much time talking about my life.

Hodges went on. "Mike discovered that Kathryn was too young to be the child in question. But I was beginning to wonder if Leah had given birth to our child, something I hadn't considered before. I had to know the truth.

"Once again, I asked Mike to help me. He has lots of contacts around the country and it wasn't hard for him to discover that a child had been born in a neighboring state to Leah Dawson in 1980 and had been adopted by the Goldmans.

"A few days ago, I learned that my biological daughter, Cece Goldman, was staying in Bellevue. For decades I had thought that Leah had carried out the abortion. I'm embarrassed to tell you I never even contacted her after she left. I closed my mind to the whole situation and moved on with what I believed was my destiny."

Hodges faced Cece again. "But I had no intention of letting you know I was aware of your existence, and I never imagined I would meet you. When John told me the names of the people who would be here today, I realized he was setting this up so that

I would finally be introduced to my own daughter. But why did you want to meet me?"

Cece's face was serene and her voice was matter-of-fact. "My parents convinced me you had a right to know you had a daughter. You see, we assumed you still believed I had been aborted." She patiently explained the story of Leah's decision to give birth to her and of the Goldmans' decision to adopt.

Cece walked over to her parents' chairs. "You should know that I have had a wonderful upbringing with two of the most loving people in the world."

Sylvia and Harry stood, one on each side of her, with their arms around her. "We don't wish to cause you any problems," Harry said.

Kate wondered if she would ever witness anything so poignant again.

Hodges's shoulders sagged. "Cece, I'm a flawed man. I'm more aware of that fact today than I ever have been before. I ask your forgiveness for what I tried to do to you."

Cece sighed deeply and looked directly at him. "I know what my parents would say, Mr. Hodges. They would tell me I should forgive anyone who asks sincerely. I don't bear a grudge, but I'm not sure I'm ready to offer forgiveness. Maybe someday, but not now."

"I understand. I may not have the right to say this, but if there's anything I can do for you, I would like to know. I don't deserve to have any part in your life, but I do hope . . ." His voice trailed off.

After another long silence, Kaplan stood. His voice had regained its usual command. "I'm sure there's a lot left to be said, but perhaps it would be best if we leave that for a future time. I'd prefer that we conclude this meeting now. If any of you need me for any reason, please let me know."

Hodges adjusted the sling on his arm, took another long look at Cece, and walked out.

Kate embraced each of the Goldmans and left.

CHAPTER 63

"**K**athryn?" Mike Strickland was sitting in the waiting room outside Kaplan's office. He stood and walked with Kate to the door. "Can we talk?" His voice caught in his throat and he coughed a couple of times.

"Hello, Mike."

He took her arm and led her out of the building to the parking lot. "I guess Bob told you I'd been getting information about you and Cece for him."

"Yes, he did."

"I want to explain. I know it may seem underhanded, but it was necessary for us to get the truth."

She stopped and looked at him. "You invited me to dinner just to find out whether or not I could have been Bob Hodges's daughter, right?"

"That's true, but I want you to know the dinner we had wasn't just about getting information. I really enjoyed being with you. It was special."

"And the photo you took of Cece at Cafe Rouge. You did that so you could show it to Hodges, didn't you?"

Mike sighed and looked at the ground. "Yes."

She started walking again. "I guess that's what politics is all about," she said indifferently. "You're very good at it, but it's not a world I want anything to do with."

They had reached her car. Kate looked back at the man who had charmed her with his smile and finesse and said, "I wish you success on the campaign. I'm sure you'll win." She reached in her purse, took out an envelope and handed it to him. "I won't be going to the inauguration." With that, she got into her car. "Good-bye, Mike."

* * *

The bandwagon is rolling and everybody's jumping on board. Mike Strickland shook his head cynically as he entered Bellevue campaign headquarters. The lethargy he had observed a couple of weeks earlier was gone, replaced by frenzied activity. Like sharks smelling blood in the water.

Jeremy looked like a bantam rooster, strutting around as if his genius had won the day. He saw Mike and raced over to gloat. "Look at this," he said as he pointed to a spreadsheet. "We're seven points up in the polls and climbing! We're gonna win!"

"That's great. Congratulations," Mike said dully. "Have you seen Bob?"

Jeremy gestured to one of the side rooms. "Yeah. He came in a few minutes ago and said he wanted some private time."

Mike found Hodges in his office, leaning back in his desk chair. He had removed the sling and was resting his right arm on his lap.

Neither man spoke as Mike moved across the room and sat down in the chair opposite the desk. There was a long silence.

Finally, Mike said, "Now what?"

"No change in plans," replied Hodges quietly. "We continue the campaign just like we intended."

"What are you going to do if they go to the press with the story?"

"I doubt they will, but if they do, I'll acknowledge the truth. No more pretending. Now, let's get Liz and Jeremy in here to review the schedule for tomorrow."

CHAPTER 64

Friday

Kate was lacing up a new pair of canary-yellow Sauconys on Friday morning when Phil called.

"Hello, beautiful."

She imagined him sitting in his office with feet propped up on his desk and that grin on his face. "Hi," she said.

"What are you doing?"

"Getting ready to take Barkley over to Campbell Park for a long run."

"After you finish, can you bring your car over to the shop? Say around one o'clock? We got that belt in, so we can install it on your car this afternoon."

"Sure, I can drop by then."

"Good. While you're here, you can pick up a little gift I have for you."

Gift? She sat on the side of her bed. *Now don't go getting all mushy. It's probably seat covers or floor mats.* "What kind of gift?"

"I can't tell you that. It's a secret."

"Sounds pretty mysterious."

"See you at one, beautiful. Be careful at the park."

She ran a strong ten miles and returned home to shower and eat before heading over to the repair shop. Phil was in his office talking with Ben Mullins when she peeked in and greeted them with a "Hi."

Phil's face registered a big smile. "Hey there. Come on in."

Both men stood up while Kate walked to the side of the desk.

Ben said, "It's good to see you, Kathryn. I swear, you get prettier every day."

Phil put his arm around her. "That's enough of that, old man. Go get your own girl."

The lines around Ben's blue eyes crinkled. "You gotta watch out for this guy, Kathryn. You can see he's the jealous type."

"Thank you, Ben. I appreciate the advice." She looked up at Phil and grinned. "I'll be careful."

"Speaking of bein' careful," Ben said, "I better get back out there and make sure those young guys don't wreck any more transmissions today." When he got to the door, he turned back with that little lopsided smile on his face. "By the way, Kathryn, who was that pretty, blonde-haired lady you were out here with last week?"

"Blonde-haired lady? You must mean my half-sister, Cece."

"Cece," he repeated. "Nice name." He sauntered out to the repair floor, whistling.

Kate raised her eyebrows. "What was that all about? Is Ben interested in Cece?"

Phil closed the office door. "Don't ask me. I'm not a mind reader, and I certainly wouldn't try to read the mind of Benjamin Herschel Mullins." He put his arms around her waist. "Besides, I don't want to talk about him."

She looked up into his face. "So, what's all this about a gift?"

"Oh, aren't we impatient?" He reached into his pocket, pulled out a key, and held it up in front of her. It had a pink ribbon tied to it with a message in white ink. "A key like a lot of other keys."

"Very funny," she said as she reached for the key.

He drew it back before she could get it. "Uh-uh. This is gonna cost you."

"You can't charge for a gift."

"Oh yeah?" He held her tight and kissed her hard; then he handed her the key. "Let's go out to the lot. If you can find the car this key belongs to, I'll give it to you."

"What, the key or the car?"

"Both."

Phil grabbed his jacket from the coat hook and they walked outside. Kate pressed the unlock button on the remote and the rear lights on a white Lexus sedan blinked. She looked at him. "That was too easy. And there's no way you're giving me a Lexus!"

They walked over to the car and she peered in. It was a real beauty and looked brand new.

"It's only a year old. The owner decided to trade down and sold it to us a few days ago. I guess it's yours. You earned it."

"You know I can't accept such an expensive automobile."

Phil put one of his hands on the side of the car, leaned in close and whispered in her ear, "It's a gift, and I won't charge you a thing. Besides, maintenance and repairs are free for as long as you own the car."

"Thanks," she smiled up at him, "but I can't do it."

Phil stood up straight again. "Seriously, Kathryn, I don't like you riding around in that old rattletrap of yours. You'd be much safer in this car."

"My car is not a rattletrap. It's a classic."

Neither of them could avoid laughing at this absurdity.

"At least use this as a loaner until we can get your car completely overhauled. Come on, let's go for a ride. Once you see how nice this one is, you might change your mind." He opened the door for her. "You drive."

She buckled in and admired the setup. "This car has everything. It's beautiful."

"I have an idea," he said as he climbed into the passenger seat. "Let's ride out to Campbell Park. You can show me the place where you and Cece met. Maybe we can take a walk while we're there."

CHAPTER 65

Kate parked in the lot next to the fencepost.

"Don't you want to consider this car now that you've driven it?" Phil asked.

"No. It drives like a dream, but I can't accept it. It's too much."

"You know, you're pretty stubborn. Your father didn't mention that when he told me about you."

"My father? What did he ever tell you about me?"

Phil took his seatbelt off and shifted in his seat to face her. "Remember I told you how your dad came in and paid a bill we had undercharged him for. He changed my life that day, but it wasn't just about his honesty. Would you like to hear the rest of it?"

"Sure."

"Your dad and I had a pretty interesting conversation that day. Most of it was about you."

"Me?"

"Yep," Phil continued. "Your dad was so proud of you. He told me how bright and wonderful you were, how you always did well in school, how you went out of your way to help students who were having trouble in math. And what a privilege it was to have such a good daughter."

Kate settled her head against the headrest. "All fathers brag about their daughters. I'm sure he made me sound a lot better than I am."

"Your father told me that some people thought of you as aloof and cool, but really you were just reserved and shy, especially around men. He said you were a very warm person, just a little hard to get to know." He reached over and pinched her in the ribs. "He didn't mention anything about the stubbornness."

Kate giggled and pushed his hand away.

"That was the conversation that changed the way I saw you. I always thought you didn't like coming to the auto shop, like it was beneath you. I guess my pride got in the way. I think your father knew I had the wrong idea about you and he wanted to straighten it out." He took her hand in his.

"So, did he straighten you out?" she teased.

"You bet he did. He said something to me that day that floored me."

"What?"

"When your dad got ready to leave, we walked out to the lot together. We got to his car and he shook my hand and looked at me with a real serious expression on his face. He said, 'You know, Phil, you'd make a great son-in-law. Maybe you should marry Kate.' Then he got in his car and drove away." Phil grinned broadly.

Kate blushed. "You're kidding me, right?"

"Nope. That's exactly what happened."

She put a hand over her face. "This is embarrassing. I knew my parents wanted me to get married, but I had no idea they were out rounding up potential husbands."

"Oh, so you think he was making this offer to other men, too?" Phil raised his eyebrows in mock surprise.

Kate laughed. "Please don't tell me he offered you a dowry."

Phil kissed her hand and looked at her with an expression that made her heart melt. "No, but I think he would have liked it if he knew you and I got to know each other better. That was the conversation that changed my life."

Kate took her seatbelt off, leaned over the console, and kissed him on the mouth. "You really know how to turn a girl's head," she said.

"I sure hope so."

They left the car and walked to the trail. Kate pointed out the fencepost where she had first seen the gold watch. As they walked along the trail, she told Phil about Cece's convincing performance as an old woman and about the dinner with the Goldmans and Mr. Kaplan that had changed her life.

When they returned to the bench, Kate said, "Three weeks ago I was an orphan, alone in the world. Today I have a sister, and the Goldmans have practically adopted me as their daughter. And I've gotten to know you. Even in this tragedy, God has blessed me."

Phil put his arms around her and held her close.

A jogger passed by and voiced his approval. "Way to go, dude."

Phil released her and said, "Have a seat on the bench and close your eyes. No peeking."

As she sat on the bench with her eyes shut, she could hear him moving around.

"Okay, you can open your eyes now."

Phil was standing in front of her with his hands stuffed in his jacket pockets. And he had that smile on his face.

She stood up and tilted her head to one side as if to say, "What's going on?"

"Oh, by the way," he said, "I have to get back to the shop soon. What time is it?"

Kate looked down at her GPS watch. "It's about three o'clock." Then she understood.

She turned and there, on top of the old fencepost was a beautiful gold watch. Its oval face was plain. No diamonds. Just tiny gold marks to indicate the hours. The wristband was made of yellow-and-white gold links. Simple and elegant. It took her breath away.

She reached over the bench, lifted the watch off the post and found an inscription on the back.

Kathryn,
Let it be me.
Phil

THE END

ABOUT THE AUTHOR

Kay DiBianca holds an MS degree in Computer Science from the University of North Carolina at Chapel Hill. She has worked in the IT departments of several major corporations, including IBM, UNC Chapel Hill, International Paper, and FedEx. Her professional experience has spanned various facets of software development, from programming to team management.

Kay and her husband, Frank, a college professor, have enjoyed many common interests over their long marriage, from flying (Kay has an instrument rating in single-engine aircraft; Frank is a glider pilot) to athletics (they both compete in the Senior Olympics, although only Kay has taken on full marathons) to their faith commitment (they are US representatives for Bridges for Peace, an international Christian organization whose mission is to serve the people of Israel and build relationships between Christians and Jews).

Kay and Frank are retired and live in Memphis, Tennessee. They have one son, Arthur, who resides in Austin, Texas.

The Watch on the Fencepost is Kay's first novel.